'You wanted honesty—well, here's honesty…' Karim said.

Suddenly Clemmie didn't want him to say anything. That frankness she had wanted now seemed so dangerous, so threatening. Yet she had pushed him to say it and she couldn't find the words to stop him. It was too late.

'I do want you.'

Karim's black eyes burned down into her wide amber ones, searing right into her thoughts.

'Never doubt it. I want you so much that it's tearing me to pieces not to have you. But what does that do for us?'

'It... You know it was an arranged marriage. One I had no part in...no agreement given. I was just a child. My father sold me!'

'The agreement is still binding. You are here to become Nabil's Queen.'

'But not yet...' she said.

Kate Walker was born in Nottinghamshire, but as she grew up in Yorkshire she has always felt that her roots are there. She met her husband at university, and originally worked as a children's librarian, but after the birth of her son she returned to her old childhood love of writing. When she's not working she divides her time between her family, their three cats, and her interests of embroidery, antiques, film and theatre—and, of course, reading.

You can visit Kate at www.kate-walker.com

Recent titles by the same author:

A THRONE FOR THE TAKING *(Royal and Ruthless)*
THE DEVIL AND MISS JONES
THE RETURN OF THE STRANGER
  (The Powerful and the Pure)
THE PROUD WIFE

A QUESTION OF HONOUR

BY
KATE WALKER

Published in Great Britain 2014
by Mills & Boon, an imprint of Harlequin (UK) Limited,
Eton House, 18-24 Paradise Road, Richmond, Surrey, TW9 1SR

© 2014 Kate Walker

ISBN: 978 0 263 90865 7

Printed and bound in Spain
by Blackprint CPI, Barcelona

A QUESTION
OF HONOUR

This book needs several dedications:

To my editor, Pippa,
whose support and understanding has been invaluable.

To Marie,
whose 'shiver down the spine' comment
told me I needed to finish it.

And to my who knows how many 'greats'
back ancestor Chevalier Charles Wogan,
whose real-life story was the inspiration
behind my fictional version.

CHAPTER ONE

'YOU KNOW WHY I'm here.'

The man's voice was as deep and dark as his eyes, his hair…his heart, for all Clemmie knew. He filled the doorway he stood in, big and broad and dangerously strong. Worryingly so.

She didn't know what put that sense of danger into his appearance. There was nothing in the way he stood, the long body relaxed, his hands pushed deep into the pockets of the well-worn jeans that clung to narrow hips and powerful legs, that spoke of threat or any sort of menace. And his face, although rough-hewn and rugged, did not have the type of features that made her think of black shadowy novels about serial killers or vampires rising from the dead.

Not that serial killers conformed to the myth that evil had to be ugly as well. And this man was definitely not ugly. He was all hunk, if the truth was told. Those deep brown eyes were combined with unbelievably luxuriant black lashes, slashing high cheekbones, surprisingly bronze-toned skin. He was a man for whom the word 'sexy' had been created. A man whose powerfully male impact went straight to everything that was female inside her and resonated there, making her shiver. But once the image of a vampire—dark, devastating and dangerous—had settled into her brain there was no way she could shake it loose.

It was something about the eyes. Something about that cold, direct, unflinching stare. Dead-eyed and unyielding. She couldn't understand it. And because she couldn't find a reason for it, it made her shiver all the more though she forced herself not to show it and instead pasted a smile that she hoped was polite but not overly encouraging on to her face.

'I beg your pardon?'

If he caught the note of rejection and dismissal she tried to inject into the words then not a sign of it registered in that enigmatic face. He certainly didn't look discouraged or even concerned but flashed her another of those cold-eyed glances and repeated, with obvious emphasis, 'You know why I'm here.'

'I think not.'

She *was* expecting someone. Had been dreading his arrival for days—weeks. Ever since the time had approached when she would celebrate her twenty-third birthday. If 'celebrated' was the right word for marking the day that would mean the end of her old life, and the start of the new. The start of the life she had known was coming but had tried to put out of her mind. Without success. The thought of what her future was to be hung over her like a dark storm cloud, blighting each day that crept nearer to the moment her destiny changed.

But she had prayed he wouldn't come so soon. That she would have at least a few more days—just a month would be perfect—before the fate that her father had planned for her when she had been too young to understand, let alone object, closed in around her and locked her into a very different existence.

The person she had been expecting—dreading—was very different from this darkly devastating male. He was much older for a start. And would never have appeared so casually dressed, so carelessly indifferent to the demands of protocol and security.

Which was just as well because the sudden and unexpected ring at the doorbell had caught her unawares. She hadn't even brushed her hair properly after washing it and letting it dry naturally, so that it hung in wild disorder around her face. Her mascara was smudged, and although she'd decided that the lipstick she'd been trying on was really too bright and garish, she hadn't had time to take any of it off, or in any way lessen the impact of the vivid colour.

'I have no idea who you are or what you're doing here. If you're selling something, I'm not interested. If you're canvassing, I'll not be voting for your party.'

'I'm not selling anything.'

No, she'd expected that. His clothes, while too obviously casual for a salesman, had a quality and style that contradicted that thought.

'Then in that case...'

She'd had enough of this. If he wasn't going to explain just why he was here then she had no intention of wasting her time standing here in the hallway. She had been busy enough before the autocratic and impatient knock had summoned her to the door and if she hung around any longer she was going to be late for Harry's party and he would never forgive her.

'I'd appreciate it if you would just leave...'

She made a move to close the door as she spoke, wanting this over and done with. Hunk or not, he had invaded her world just at the worst possible moment.

She had so little time to spare. Correction—she had no time to spare. No time at all for herself, no time between her and the future, the fate that had once seemed so far away. She had to finish packing, organise the legal transfer of the cottage and everything else she was leaving behind. And that was always supposing that she could persuade the man she really was waiting for to give her just two days more grace.

Just forty-eight more hours. It would mean so little to him, except as a delay in the mission he'd been sent on, but it would mean the world to her—and to Harry. A tiny bubble of tension lurched up into her throat and burst there painfully as she thought about the promise she had made to Harry just the previous evening.

'I'll be there, sweetheart, I promise. I won't let anything stand in my way.'

And she wouldn't, she had vowed. She had just enough time to visit Harry, be with him through this special time, and then make it back home. Back to face the fate she now knew her dreams of escaping would never ever come true. Back to face the prospect of a future that had been signed away from her with the dictates of a peace treaty, the plans of other people so much more powerful than she could ever be. The only thing that made it bearable was the knowledge that Harry would never be trapped as she had been. Her father knew nothing about him, and she would do anything rather than let him find out.

But that had been before she had received the unwelcome news that the visitor she so dreaded seeing would be here much sooner than she had anticipated. Forty-eight hours earlier. The vital forty-eight hours she needed.

And now here was this man—this undeniably gorgeous but totally unwelcome man—invading what little was left of her privacy, and holding her up when she needed to be on her way.

'Leave right now,' she added, the uneasy feelings in her mind giving more emphasis to her words, a hard-voiced stress that she would never have shown under any other circumstances. As she spoke she moved to shut the door, knowing a nervous need to slam it into its frame, right in his face. That feeling was mixed with a creeping, disturbing conviction that if she didn't get rid of him now, once and for all, he was going to ruin her plans completely.

'I think not.'

She only just heard his low-toned words under her own sharp gasp of shock as the door hit against some unexpected blockage at its base. She suddenly became disturbingly aware of the way that he had moved forward, sudden and silent as a striking predator, firmly inserting one booted foot between the wood and its frame. A long, strong fingered hand flashed out to slam into it too, just above her head, holding it back with an ease that denied the brutal force he was employing against her own pathetic attempt at resistance. The shock of the impact ricocheted disturbingly up her arm.

'I think not,' he repeated, low and dangerous. 'I'm not going anywhere.'

'Then you'd better think again!' she tossed at him in open defiance, her head going back, bronze eyes flashing golden sparks of rejection.

He'd expected problems, Karim Al Khalifa acknowledged to himself. The way that this woman had taken herself off from the court, the sort of life she had set up for herself, ignoring all demands of protocol and safety, in a different country, all indicated that this was not going to be the straightforward task his father had led him to believe. Clementina Savanevski—or Clemmie Savens, which was the name she was masquerading under in this rural English hideaway—knew where her duty lay, or she should do. But the fact that she had run away from that duty, and had been living a carefree life on her own had always indicated that she held her family's promise very lightly. Far too lightly.

And now that he was face to face with her, he felt he understood why.

She had clearly cast off the restraint and the dignity she should be expected to have as a potential Queen of Rhastaan. She had on only a loose, faded tee shirt and shabby denim jeans, the latter so battered that they were actually threadbare in places where they clung to her tall, slender figure. The long dark hair hung wild around her face, tumbling down on to her shoulders and back in a disarray that was as shocking as it was sensual. Her face was marked with dark smudges around her deep amber eyes, a garish crimson lipstick staining her mouth.

And what a mouth.

Unexpectedly, shockingly, his senses seemed to catch on the thought, his heart lurching sharply, making his breath tangle inside his chest so that for a second he felt he would never exhale again. His own mouth burned as if it had made contact with the red-painted fullness of hers, his tongue moving involuntarily to sweep over his lower lip in instinctive response.

'I'll call the police!'

She moved back to her place by the door so that she was blocking his way if he wanted to come towards her.

The movement drew his attention to her feet on the wooden floor. Long, elegant, golden-skinned, they were tipped with an astonishingly bright pink polish on her nails. And the movement had brought a waft of some tantalising perfume stirring on the air. Flowers, but with an unexpected undertone of sexy spice.

'No need for that.' His voice was rough around the edges as he had to push it from an unexpectedly dry throat. 'I'm not going to hurt you.'

'And you expect me to believe that, do you?' she challenged, flinging another furious and flashing glare into his face.

Knowing she had caught his attention, she let her gaze drop downwards in a deliberate move to draw his attention to where his foot still came between the door and its white-painted frame, blocking the way.

'Does that look like *normal* behaviour?' she questioned roughly, nodding towards the carefully imposed barrier. Her tone was almost as raw as his but for very different reasons, he suspected. She was furious, practically spitting her anger at him. And suddenly he had the image in his head of a young, thin stray cat he had seen in a car park only that morning. A sleek black beauty who had started in violent apprehension when he had approached it and, turning, had hissed its defiance in his face.

He was handling this all wrong, Karim acknowledged uncomfortably. Somewhere in the moments between the time he had arrived here and she had answered the door, all his carefully planned tactics had gone right up in smoke and he had taken completely the wrong approach. He hadn't expected her to be so hostile, so defiant. Raw and unsettled as he was already with thoughts of the situation he had left behind at home, worry about his father's health, the way he had been forced so unexpectedly into taking this action today, he had let his usual rigid control slip shamefully.

That and the fact that he'd been without a woman for so long, he acknowledged unwillingly. Too long. There had been no one in his bed or even near it since Soraya had stormed out, accusing him of never being there for her. Never being there, full stop. Well, of course he hadn't. When had he had the time, or the freedom of thought, to be there for anyone other than his father, or the country that he now found himself so brutally and unexpectedly heir to? The problems that had flared up so suddenly had taken every second of his time, forcing him to take on his father's duties as well as his own. He wouldn't be here otherwise. Not willingly.

And, face it, he had never expected her to be so physically gorgeous. So incredibly sexy. He had seen photographs of her, of course, but not a single one of those pictures had the sensual impact of the molten bronze eyes, golden skin, tousled black hair and the intoxicating scent that seemed to have tangled itself around his nerves, pulling tight. His mouth almost watered, his senses burning to life in the space of a heartbeat.

No.

Hastily, he pulled himself up. He couldn't allow thoughts like that to sneak into his mind, even for a moment. It didn't matter a damn if this woman was the sexiest female on earth—and he refused to listen to his senses' insistence that that might just be the case—she was not for him. She was *forbidden* to him, dammit. They were on opposite sides of a huge divide and, frankly, it was better it stayed that way. From what he had heard, she was too much trouble to be worth any transient pleasure. And he already had too much on his conscience as it was.

'My apologies,' he said stiffly, imposing control on his voice in the hope that the rest of his senses would follow. 'I am not going to hurt you.'

'Do you think that if you say it often enough I'll be forced to believe you?' she challenged. 'What's that phrase about protesting too much?'

He wasn't sure if she had deliberately flung the question at him to distract him, but it worked. Puzzled, he reacted without thinking, taking his foot from the door and, sensing the lessening of pressure against her hand, she acted instinctively, pushing the door back against him and whirling away from him, dashing back inside the house.

If she could just reach the phone, she could call the police, Clemmie told herself. Or she could hope to get right through the house and out of the back door. She didn't trust for one minute his declaration that he had no intention of hurting her. He meant trouble, she was sure. Some deeply primitive instinct told her that, gorgeous or not, he was dangerous right through to the bone.

But she hadn't pushed the door quite soon enough. She knew the moment that he stopped it from closing, the silence instead of the bang of wood on wood. He had stepped into the hallway; was right behind her. Every nerve, every muscle tensed in anticipation of his coming to claim her, to grab at her shoulder or her arms. But, unbelievably, as she dashed into the kitchen she heard him come to a halt.

'Clementina.'

Whatever she had expected, it wasn't that. Wasn't the use of her name—her full name. The one that no one here in England used. The one that no one even knew *was* her real name. And the sound of it stopped her dead, freezing her into stillness in the middle of her tiny kitchen.

'Clementina—please.'

Please? Now she had to be hearing things. He couldn't have said that. He wouldn't have said *please*—would he?

'I'm not coming any further,' he said with careful control. 'I'm going to stay here and we should talk. Let me explain—my name is Karim Al Khalifa.'

Through the buzzing in her head, Clemmie heard the words so differently. She had been expecting to hear that name, or one so very like it, that she believed he'd said what she'd anticipated.

'Now I know you're lying.'

She tossed the words over her shoulder, turning her head just far enough to see that he had actually halted as he had said, just outside the kitchen door.

'I don't know how you know that I was waiting for someone to come here from Sheikh Al Khalifa, but it sure as blazes wasn't you. I've seen a picture of the man who was coming and he's at least twice your age, has a beard. The photo's on my computer—it was in the email…'

'Was,' he inserted, cold and sharp. 'The important word there is "was".'

'What *are* you talking about?'

Needing to see him to look into his face, meet his eyes, to try and read just what was going on inside his handsome head, she made herself turn to confront him and immediately wished she hadn't. The dark glaze of his eyes was like black ice, making her stomach lurch. At the same time she felt the clench of her nerves in another, very different sort of response. A very female, very sensual sort of reaction. One that made her throat ache in a way that had nothing to do with fear.

One that was the last thing she wanted, or should even acknowledge she was feeling.

'The man who *was* coming,' he repeated with a dark emphasis. 'But isn't any more.'

'And how do you know…' Clemmie began, only to find that her voice failed her, the rest of the question fading away into an embarrassing squeak. This man knew too much about her situation—but from what sources?

Suddenly, she was nervous in a new way. One that had thoughts of diplomacy, peace treaties, international situations and strong tensions between countries running through her head. Her hands felt damp and she ran them down the sides of her thighs to ease the sensation, her heart clenching painfully as she watched his dark eyes drop to follow the betraying movement.

His eyes lingered in a way that made her shift uncomfortably from one foot to another on the terracotta-tiled floor.

'I know because I organised it,' was the emotionless response. 'My father ordered what was to happen and instructed Adnan to come and fetch you. He also had the photo of the man he'd put in charge of this sent to you so that you knew who was coming. At least those were the original arrangements—but then everything changed.'

'Changed?'

It felt as if her blood was weakening, the strength seeping out of her so that she almost imagined there would be a damp pool collecting on the floor at her feet. Adnan was the name of the man Sheikh Al Khalifa had said he would send. The man who was to see her safe to Rhastaan. And she needed her safety to be guaranteed.

Not everyone was as pleased about this prospective marriage as her father. Sheikh Ankhara, whose lands bordered Rhastaan, and who had always wanted the throne for his own daughter, had made no secret of the fact that he would sabotage it if he could. It was because of a possible threat from him that Sheikh Al Khalifa—*my father,* Karim had said—had taken charge, organising a trusted man to escort her to Nabil.

But now Karim was saying that he had changed those arrangements. Did that mean that something had gone wrong?

'Do you want to sit down?'

Her feelings must have shown in her face. Perhaps the blood had drained from there too.

'Here.'

He had crossed to the sink, snatching up a glass and filling it with water from the tap.

'Take this…'

He pushed it into her hand then closed his own hand around hers as her shockingly nerveless fingers refused to grasp it, coming dangerously close to letting it drop and smash on the tiles.

'Drink it.' It was a command as he lifted the glass to her lips.

She managed a little sip, struggling to swallow even the small amount of water. He was so shockingly close. If she breathed in she could inhale the scent of his skin, the faint tang of some aromatic aftershave. His hands were warm on hers, sending pulses of reaction over her skin, and if she looked up into his dark eyes she could see herself reflected in their depths, a tiny, pale-faced thing with huge eyes that gave away too much. She didn't like how the image made her feel diminished in a way that was as powerful as her awareness of the force and strength of the long body so close to hers, creating a pounding turmoil inside her head.

'Your—did you say your father?'

A sharp, curt nod of that dark head was his only response. He was still holding the glass of water to her lips, not pushing it at her, but making it plain that he believed she needed more. It was a toss-up between easing the painful tightness of her throat or risking making herself sick as she struggled to swallow.

She managed another sip then pushed the glass away. The brief slick of her tongue over her lips did little to ease the way she was feeling. Particularly not when she saw that darkly intent gaze drop to follow the small movement and she actually saw the kick of his pulse at the base of his throat. Was it possible that he was feeling something of the same heated reaction as the one that had seared through her at his touch?

'And who, precisely, is your father?'

'You know his name—you talked of him just now.'

'I talked of Sheikh Al Khalifa, but he can't...' Another nod, as sharp and hard as the first, cut her off in midsentence and she had to shake her head violently, sending her dark hair flying as she tried to deny what he was saying. 'No—he can't... Prove it!'

A faint shrug of those broad shoulders dismissed her challenge but all the same he reached into his jacket pocket, pulled out a wallet and flipped it open, holding it up in front of her.

'My name is Karim Al Khalifa,' he said slowly and carefully, as if explaining to a difficult and not very bright child. 'Shamil Al Khalifa is my father—he is also the man whose envoy you were expecting. Isn't he?' he demanded when she could only stare at the driving licence, the bank cards in blank silence.

'But if he—' Clemmie shook her head slowly, unable to take it all in. 'Why would he send you—his *son*...?'

Because if this Karim was the Sheikh's son then that meant he must be a prince in his own right, as rich and powerful—possibly more so—as Nabil, who was the reason for this situation in the first place.

'I was expecting a member of his security team. Someone who would make sure that I travelled safely to Rhastaan and...'

'And met up with your prospective groom,' Karim finished for her, making it clear that he really did know all about the situation; that he was well aware of what was going on.

'Things made it—imperative—that the arrangement we'd put in place could not go ahead as we planned. Plans had to be changed at the last moment.'

'But why?'

'Because it was necessary.'

And that was all the explanation she was going to get, Clemmie was forced to acknowledge as Karim pushed himself upright, straightening his long back and flexing his broad shoulders. He strode to the sink, tossed what was left of the water into it and placed the glass on the draining board. The air around Clemmie suddenly felt uncomfortably cold without the warm strength of his body so close to hers.

'And those plans mean that we don't have any time to waste.' He flung the words over his shoulder, not even troubling to turn and face her as he spoke. 'I hope you've packed as instructed, because we have to leave now.'

'Now?' That brought her to her feet in a rush. *As instructed.* Who did he think he was?

'No way. That's not happening.'

'Oh, but I assure you that it is.'

She'd planned on arguing against this. Or, at the very least, she'd hoped to discuss it with the man who was due to arrive at her cottage. Her birthday was still nine days away. Less than a month, but that made all the difference.

'The contract that was drawn up between my family and the rulers of Rhastaan only comes into effect on December third. The day I turn twenty-three.'

'That day will come soon enough. We'll be in Rhastaan by the time you come of age.'

So he did know everything about her. Was it supposed to reassure, to let her know that he really was in control of the situation? Because reassure was the last thing it did. She had known that one day someone would come for her. It had been decided, signed and sealed thirteen years before, when the son of the Sheikh of Rhastaan was five, and she not quite ten. They had been betrothed, contracted to each other, to be married when Nabil reached adulthood. She had had some years of freedom, time to complete a university course, while their parents waited for her prospective husband to become old enough to wed and to hold the throne of his own kingdom. And now that time was up.

But not yet. Please, not yet.

Clemmie had thought that she would be able to argue with the man who had been sent. That she could at least pull rank just a little, insist on having a day or two's grace before she had to leave. The man she had thought was coming to collect her—an older man, a *family* man, she had hoped—might be someone she could appeal to.

Someone who would give her that breathing space and let her have a chance of fulfilling her promise to Harry.

But this dark, sleek, dangerous panther of a man—would he listen to a word she had to say? Would he give her any sort of chance? She doubted it. Especially when she couldn't tell him—or anyone—the whole truth. She didn't dare. It was vital that she kept Harry's existence a total secret. If anyone ever found out about him then the little boy's future was at risk.

So how could she persuade him?

'I need more time. A few days.'

You have to be joking, the look he turned on her said without words. It made her feel like some small, crawling insect just within crushing reach of his feet in their highly polished handmade shoes. A small, crawling *female* insect. And from the way he looked down his straight slash of a nose, the burn of contempt in the blackness of his eyes, she knew just which of those words he considered to be the greatest possible insult he could toss her way.

She made herself face him, her eyes locking with his, burning with the defiance she felt towards his arrogant decree.

'And who precisely are you to order me around?'

'I told you—I am Karim Al Khalifa, Crown Prince of Markhazad.'

He obviously thought that his cold statement would impress her but he couldn't be more wrong. She'd spent so much time as she grew up with the royal family who were destined to be her family one day. It had been a sterile, regimented existence, with very few moments of freedom. Her father had been determined that she knew how to behave, how to follow court protocol. She had been trained for her role. When she married they would be more than equals, and soon she would be queen.

'Crown Prince, hmm? So why are you here, running errands—'

He hadn't liked that, not one bit. A flame of anger had flared in those polished jet eyes, turning them from ice to fire in the space of a heartbeat. And, contradictorily, that chilled her own blood till she felt it might freeze in her veins.

'I am here representing my father,' he snapped, cutting her off before she could complete the sentence. 'Not running errands. And as my father's representative I insist that you pack your bags and get ready to leave.'

'You can insist all you like. I've no intention of going anywhere with you so I suggest you just turn around and walk out that door.'

'And I have no intention of leaving—at least, not without you.'

How could that gorgeous, sensual mouth make a simple statement sound like the most terrible threat since time began? And the husky appeal of his accent only added to the horror of the contradiction.

'I've come for you. And I'm leaving with you. And that is all there is to it.'

CHAPTER TWO

Was she really going to make this more difficult than he had ever thought? Karim found it hard to believe that this slip of a girl was going to make things so very problematic for him.

And the worst part of it was that he couldn't even tell her the truth. He couldn't reveal to her just what was behind his coming here, the problems and dangers that had meant he had to deal with this himself, rather than leave it to Adnan who, although a member of the security team, was not the right man for the job. Definitely not once Karim had found out that he was secretly in the pay of Ankhara.

His eyes narrowed as he looked into Clementina's face assessingly, wondering just how much he could tell her. How much did she know about Sheikh Ankhara and his ambitions to put his own daughter on the throne of Rhastaan? Karim had no doubt that if Adnan had been the one to collect her, as had originally been planned, then there would have been some unfortunate 'accident' on the journey back. Anything to ensure that she didn't make it to her wedding.

Clementina didn't look like the type of delicate flower who would go into some sort of emotional meltdown if she realised the risks involved in getting her out of here and taking her back to Rhastaan, handing her over to her husband-to-be. On the contrary, she had been hissing and spitting defiance at him ever since he had arrived, like some beautiful, hostile, wild cat that had been driven into a corner and trapped there, her back against the wall. And just because she was sleek-boned and soft-haired, he would be all sorts of a fool if he let himself think of her as any sort of kitten rather than a fully grown cat. She was far more likely to lash out and scratch him viciously if he tried to touch her, rather than purring and preening under his caress.

Just for a moment the thought of her arching that elegant back to meet his hands, or rubbing the softness of her hair against his face made his breath knot in his throat, his blood heating as his body tightened in the sort of purely carnal hunger he hadn't known for some time.

Hell, no! This was not the way he had expected to feel about this woman. It was the last thing he should feel about the betrothed bride of the young King of Rhastaan. It went against all the laws of honour and trust. It threatened the reasons why he was here right down to the very roots that had founded them. It was why he had had to move away from her earlier, when the purely instinctive move to offer her a drink of water had suddenly turned into some sort of brutal sensual endurance test. He hadn't been able to stay there, so close that he could feel the warmth of her body, see the pulse of her blood beating blue under the fine skin at the base of her throat. When she moved, some delicate scent had slipped into the air and combined with the soft brush of a wandering strand of her dark silky hair across his face, which caught on the roughness of the day's growth of dark stubble to create a burn of response that was almost more than he could endure.

Suddenly he wanted her so much that it hurt. He had never wanted a woman so much and yet she was the last woman he could ever, should ever feel that way about. She was not available; not for him.

She was *forbidden* to him.

So the best damn thing that he could do was get her out of here, on the jet where she would be safe and hidden again, on their way to Rhastaan, and deliver her to her bridegroom just as soon as he possibly could.

'So—are you going to pack?' he demanded, his voice rough with all that he was fighting to hold back.

He wouldn't even meet her eyes though he could tell that was what she wanted. She sought to confront him face to face, challenging everything he said.

Was she really so irresponsible, so careless of the consequences of her actions, that she would defy him out of sheer perversity? That she would put everything so many people had worked towards in jeopardy on a selfish whim? She had been given a touch of, if not freedom, then at least the chance to run on an exceptionally loose rein for a while. But even the most magnificent thoroughbred was the better for a little restraint, a strong grip on the bridle, a light touch of spurs, to keep it under control. Clementina Savanevski, soon to be Queen Clementina of Rhastaan, could not be allowed to run wild any more. And if anyone could be relied on to bring her under control then he was the man to do it. That was one of the reasons why his father had sent him on this mission in the first place.

'Well?'

'I am packed,' she surprised him—stunned him—by

saying. He had been expecting further defiance, further rebellion. In fact, if he was honest he was actually a touch disappointed that she wasn't digging in her neat little heels, bringing up that small chin once more and letting her glorious amber eyes clash with his in pure defiance. He'd expected it, and anticipated the thrill of battle that would come from bringing her back under control.

'You are? Then it's time…'

'But not to leave here,' she disconcerted him by adding. 'I've only packed an overnight bag.'

'That won't be adequate.' She knew that; why was he even having to say it? 'You need to pack everything you want to take with you. You'll not be coming back here again.'

'Oh, but there you're wrong.'

Something had set her soft mouth into a surprisingly hard determined line, and the way she shook her head sent the dark hair flying again, tormenting his nostrils with that subtle floral scent.

'I'm only going away for one night this time—and then I will be back. I'll do my proper packing then. Look…' she broke in hastily when he opened his mouth to reject her outrageous statement and tell her just what he thought of such stupidity '…I can explain.'

'You can try,' Karim growled, fighting the urge to grab her by the arms, bundle her out of the door, into his car and drive away from here just as quickly as he could. That would meet one of the demands of this mission and get her on the road back to Rhastaan as soon as he could.

But it would also defeat the other part of the plan, which was to move her from A to B with as little fuss and publicity as possible. If he virtually kidnapped her—because that would be how she would interpret his actions—

then she would react strongly, possibly go into meltdown and panic completely. She would certainly not go quietly—not this woman. If she started screaming for help or calling for the police, even here in this small village, she would soon draw too much unwanted attention to who they were and where they were going.

'You're not going anywhere. Not for one night—not for any time at all.'

'But… Please…'

Hastily, she seemed to adjust her frame of mind, altering her tone to match so that it was suddenly disturbingly soft and cajoling. Obviously, she had decided to try to entice him round to her way of thinking. And the shocking thing was the way that just hearing that low, almost gentle tone changed his mood. He wanted to hear more of that voice, could imagine it murmuring to him in bed, whispering temptation in the heated darkness of his room. And that was not an image he needed in his mind right now.

'Haven't you ever wanted—needed—to keep a promise? So much so that you would do anything at all to make sure you did just that?'

'What?' His brows drew together in a dark frown. 'Of course I have.' It was why he was here now. 'But…'

'Then you'll know exactly how I'm feeling right now. I made a promise…'

'To whom?'

'To Har—to someone,' she corrected hastily, obviously horrified that she had almost blurted out the truth. 'Someone who really matters to me.'

She had been about to give someone's name. A man's? *Harry? Someone who really matters to me.*

'Nothing matters—' Karim's tone was harsh and

unyielding. His face seemed carved from stone, not a muscle moving to reveal any sympathy or understanding. 'Nothing should matter more than the promises you made—your commitment to Nabil.'

'I know all about my *commitment* to Nabil and, believe me, I mean—' Something caught in her throat, making the words tangle there, tight as a knot, so that she had to struggle to force them out. 'I mean to honour it.'

She had no choice. None at all. Not unless she wanted to risk the ruin of international relations between two powerful kingdoms. The possible outbreak of hostilities. The destruction of her family's reputation. Hadn't her father drummed it into her from the moment he had signed the documents? He had made it sound as if it was her sacred duty. She had been fifteen before she'd realised just how much he was getting out of it himself, that the luxury they lived in had been bought from the sale of his own daughter.

'But not yet.'

'You will be twenty-three in nine days' time.' Could his voice be any more cold, any more inflexible? 'You do not have any more time to delay. You've had your freedom, been let off the leash for a while; now it is time to consider your duty.'

'Consider my duty!'

Clemmie threw up her hands in a gesture that was a blend of exasperation and despair.

'Do you think I've ever done anything else? That I've ever been able to forget it?'

'Then you will know why...' Karim put in, but she ploughed on, unable to hold back any longer.

'And *let off the leash*! You make me sound like a naughty puppy dog that has to be brought to heel.'

If the cap fits… his expression said. That was all she was in his eyes. A naughty, disobedient puppy who had been running wild for far too long. She could almost see him snapping his fingers and declaring 'Heel—now!'

She had not been able to tell anyone why she had wanted to leave Markhazad in the first place. She had had to go, while she still could. Once she was married, once she was queen, her life would be lived within the confines of the palace walls, subject to her husband's control, his to command. And she would have lost her last chance to spend time with the only other member of her family. The little boy who had now stolen her heart completely.

'You are to be a queen,' Karim said now, his tone dark and disapproving. 'You should learn to behave like one.'

'Unlike my mother?' Clemmie challenged.

Everyone who knew of her story must know how her English mother had run away from the court, leaving husband and daughter behind, never to be seen again. Clemmie winced away from the memory of how it had felt to be left alone, abandoned by her one defender from her father's worst excesses. Those had been the worst years of her life. It was only recently, in the letter from her maternal grandmother that had been delivered to her after the old lady had died, that she had learned why her mother had had to run. The unplanned, late in life baby she had been determined to hide from her husband. He was a secret that Clemmie was now just as determined to keep, whatever it cost her.

She knew how little her father had valued her because she was only a daughter. She had no needs or dreams of her own. Her only value to him had been in the marriage market, sold to the highest bidder. What he might have done if he knew he had the son he had dreamed of made her shudder to think.

'I'll behave like one when I am a queen! Until then...'

She watched that frown darken, felt a shiver run over her scalp and slither down her spine. She had a suspicion that she knew what he was thinking but she didn't dare challenge it in case it meant he subjected her to more questioning that might push her to drop something revealing about Harry and his circumstances.

'There is no "until then". From this moment on you are the prospective Queen of Rhastaan, and I have been sent to fetch you home for your wedding and then your coronation.'

'But I promised! And if he...'

'He...' Karim pounced on the word like a cat on a mouse, his eyes gleaming with the thrill of the chase. '*He*. Just who is he?'

Clemmie bit down hard on her lower lip in distress at how close she had come to giving herself away. She should know better. Even after less than half an hour in this man's company, it was obvious that he was not the sort of person who was easily side-tracked or misled.

'N-no one. Just a friend. Someone I met while I was living here in England. It's his birthday soon and I promised him I'd be at his party.'

What was it they said—that if you were going to lie, then lie as close to the truth as you possibly could? He was focused on her so completely that she had little hope of getting away from him...unless...

'And you think that you can delay our journey—the plans for the reception and the wedding that are already underway—for a *party*?'

'But I promised! It'll break his heart...'

'And you expect me to believe that?' Dark eyes turned glacial as he flung the question at her. 'Just because you're about to become a princess doesn't mean that I have to believe in the fairy tales you make up.'

'It's not a fairy tale. I have to see—to see…' The realisation of the danger in giving away just what she had to do dried her mouth and had the words shrivelling up into silence.

'You have to see…?' Karim queried cynically. 'Just what is more important than the upcoming wedding— the future of the peace treaty?'

My family. My baby brother. *Harry.* The words beat inside her head, creating a terrible clenching sensation in her stomach that made her feel both nauseous and dry-mouthed in the same moment. A deadly combination.

But at the back of her mind there was the idea that had come to her like a flash of inspiration just moments before. It might just work. And she was desperate enough to try anything.

'Who is this man—your lover?'

That was just so ridiculous that she was close to laughing out loud. Did he really think that she had come to England to meet up with a man? But perhaps it might almost be worth letting him think that for now. At least it would distract him from the truth. And while he was distracted…

'Oh, okay! You win.' She hoped it sounded yielding enough. 'It seems I have no choice so I'll go and get my bag. Look, why don't you make a coffee or something? If we're going to have to travel, we might as well have a drink before we go.'

He still eyed her with suspicion and he didn't show any sign of moving towards the kettle as she walked past him and made her way up the stairs, her feet thumping on the uncarpeted wood. She walked noisily across the floor of her small bedroom, the one that was to the left off the landing, thankfully not the one directly above the kitchen. She had no doubt that Karim Al Khalifa was still standing, alert as a predatory hunter, listening to any sounds that reached him from above.

Determinedly, she added to the sound effects he would be waiting to hear by banging open the door of the elderly pine wardrobe, rattling the coat hangers inside. There was really no need to do any such thing. The small overnight bag she had prepared earlier was still lying, full and firmly zipped up, on the bed. But Karim would be expecting her to pack more than that. He thought she was leaving with him for ever. For the rest of her life.

The thought made her rattle some more coat hangers even more viciously, wishing she could throw some of them at Karim's handsome head.

Karim Al Khalifa. The name reverberated in her head, making her pause to think. He was the son of the Sheikh—a friend of Nabil's late father—who had arranged all this. So why had someone so important—the Crown Prince, after all—come on a mission like this? He had never explained that.

'Clementina?'

Karim's voice, sharp with impatience, came up the narrow staircase. He had clearly noted her silence. And he just as clearly wanted to be on his way. He wouldn't be prepared to wait much longer.

'Nearly done!' She hoped her unconcerned tone was convincing. 'Be down in a minute.'

She had to be out of here. Grabbing the small overnight bag and slinging its longer strap around her neck, and grabbing her handbag, she crept over to the half-open window. Karim might be big and strong and powerful but she had the advantage over him here. Several childhood holidays in England, visiting her English grandmother, had given her a detailed knowledge of this old house and the secret ways in and out of it that had been fun and exciting for a tomboyish teenager.

There was a trellis up the side of the wall, a heavy rich growth of ivy that was thick and strong enough to support her weight even though she was now no longer thirteen and just growing into her womanly form. With luck she could scramble down it, get to her car before he had even realised she had gone silent in the room above him.

But as she eased the window open fully, a last minute thought struck her. This wasn't just a personal thing; there were so many other implications of all this—political ones, international treaties. If she just disappeared then, she shivered at the thought of the trouble it might cause. The repercussions of her behaviour. On her country. On him.

There was a notepad and pen beside her bed and she snatched these up, scribbling down five hasty words, adding her signature as an afterthought.

'Clementina!'

What little patience Karim had was wearing thin.

'Just a minute—or would you like to come and pack for me?' she challenged.

The thought of him doing just that—coming upstairs, into her room, into her *bedroom*—made her heart lurch up into her throat, snatching her breath from her. But his growled response made her feel more relaxed.

'Get on with it then.'

'Oh, I will!'

Leaving the note lying in the middle of the bed where he couldn't possibly miss it, she edged towards the window, her bare feet silent on the floor, her bag on one arm. She didn't dare risk opening the window any further in case it creaked, the wood scraping against wood.

Sliding out backwards, her feet found the spaces in the trellis work that held the ivy tight against the wall with the ease of long-held memory. She prayed it would still hold her—they were both ten years older, herself and the criss-crossed wood. And she was definitely inches taller, pounds heavier. Her toes found the footholds, her hands knowing just where to grab to support herself on the way down. Holding her breath, she let the ivy take all her weight, inched her way down the wall, down to the ground at the back of the cottage, landing with a small sigh of relief as her feet touched the gravel.

'So far so good…'

Her battered red Mini was parked several metres away, its small size and well-worn paintwork totally overshadowed by the big black beast of a SUV that was drawn up just outside the front door. A car as sleek and powerful as the man himself, Clemmie told herself as she wrenched the driver's door open, tossed the bags on to the back seat, flinging herself after them and pushing her key into the ignition almost before she was settled.

The moment that the Mini's engine roared into life was her last chance. Karim had to hear it and would come running so it was now or never. Not even bothering to fasten her seat belt—that could come later—she let off the brake, pushed her foot down on the accelerator and set the car off down the drive at breakneck speed.

She thought she saw the flash of movement—the opening of the door—the appearance of a tall, dark, powerful figure in the empty space, but she didn't take the time to be sure. She needed to focus on the road ahead.

'I'm coming, Harry!'

Pieces of gravel spurted up from under her car's tyres as she headed for the lane and, after that, the motorway and freedom.

At least for now.

CHAPTER THREE

THE SNOW THAT had been threatening from the moment she'd woken up was falling steadily by the time that Clemmie turned off the motorway and headed back to the village. Huge white flakes whirled in front of her windscreen and the elderly wipers had trouble pushing them aside so that she could see the road.

'Oh, come on!' she muttered out loud, concentrating fiercely on steering as carefully as possible. After just over nine months in England, and most of that spent in much warmer and easier weather conditions, she was unused to driving over icy roads, and the addition of the slippery coating of snow made the situation even more treacherous.

Added to that, her elderly car was not exactly in the best state for difficult weather driving. Because she had basically run away from home when she had found out about Harry, not taking much money with her, and not wanting to use her bank cards in case someone found where she was staying, she had bought the cheapest, oldest car she could afford. A decision that had seemed wise at the time, but which she was really regretting now.

Particularly when the engine started to splutter in a worrying way, and the rather worn tyres spun on the frozen surface. If only she had the sort of powerful, brand new four-wheel drive that had brought Karim to the cottage. That beast would have eaten up the miles between the small market town where Harry lived and the moorland village where she had made her temporary home with no trouble.

'Karim.'

Just the thought of him took her attention so that her concentration on her driving went along with it. For a couple of dangerous seconds, the car drifted towards the centre of the road, only coming back under control as she shook her head sharply, reminding herself of where she was.

But the thought of coming face to face with Karim once again made her stomach nerves tighten and twist into painful knots.

Karim Al Khalifa would be waiting for her when she got home. OK, perhaps he wouldn't actually be in the house, but she knew that as soon as he realised she was back, he would be there on the doorstep once again, demanding that she come with him, travel with him back to Rhastaan.

And to her wedding.

Once again the wheel jerked under her convulsive grip, and the unpleasant groaning sound that came from the engine made her wince in distress.

There was no avoiding it now. No hope of gaining any more time or hoping for a reprieve. Her twenty-third birthday was coming up fast, and Nabil had come of age last month. The promises their parents had made to each other would have to be kept. The marriage that had been arranged all those years before must now take place. Or the consequences were unthinkable.

And Karim had been sent to make sure that she kept her word.

Just for a moment the image of Nabil as she had last seen him floated behind her eyes. A gangling youth—not much more than a boy, with hooded eyes, a whisper of a moustache under his hooked nose and a sullen mouth, and her stomach clenched on a pang of nerves. But perhaps he had changed, grown up in the time since she had been at the court. He would be a year older after all.

And it was really rather unfair to consider him in the same thought as Karim Al Khalifa. Karim, the dark and devastating. Karim, with the tall and muscular frame that dominated a room so effortlessly. With the sexy, deep-toned voice, the powerful yet somehow elegant hands, the polished jet eyes and the stunning, outrageously lush thick lashes that framed them.

'What am I doing?'

Clemmie's hands tightened round the steering wheel until her knuckles showed white.

Up ahead, on the horizon at the top of the hill, almost concealed by the wildly whirling snow, the outline of the cottage appeared etched against the heavy grey-whiteness of the sky. Home. Or it should have felt like home, like coming back to safety, warmth and comfort after the long and difficult journey.

This little cottage had been the only sort of home she had ever known. Holidays with her English grandmother had given her a tiny taste of freedom from the rules and protocol of the court. Used to the burning heat of Balakhar and Rhastaan, she had loved the peace and quiet, the green fields that surrounded it, the sweeping view spread out from where it stood high on the hill. She had lived a much simpler, very different way of life with her grandmother, how different she hadn't fully realised until she had seen the happy, relaxed childhood Harry was now enjoying with his adoptive parents. They might not have anything like the luxuries she had known but they had one great treasure—the love they shared. And the freedom she was determined to preserve for Harry at all costs.

But the cottage no longer felt like home. Instead, it seemed as if she was heading foolishly into a trap, putting her head into the lion's jaws. And the sleek, dark predator who had turned her home into an alien, hostile environment was Karim Al Khalifa.

But the problem was that she wasn't thinking of him as that predator. She wasn't even remembering him as the cold-eyed, tight-jawed, arrogant representative of the Sheikh of Markhazad. The Crown Prince of Markhazad himself. All she could focus on right now was the man himself.

And what a man.

Shivering pulses of excitement sparked along her nerves at just the memory, the recollection of having him so close, the scent of his skin. He was not a man to be alone with in the confined space of her small cottage. He was pure temptation, and tempted was something she couldn't afford to be—not now, not ever.

Just for a second Clemmie considered putting the car into a turn and heading back the way she had come. Back to the house where she had just left Harry, so happy and secure, worn out after the excitement and enjoyment of his birthday party. Surely Arthur and Mary Clendon, Harry's adoptive parents, would give her support, somewhere to stay…

'No!'

She couldn't go back on her word. The word she had

given to her father and the Sheikh. However much she felt her insides twist in apprehension at the thought of the future, she had made her promise and she had to stick by it. If she didn't, then someone else would come looking for her—after all, Karim had found her easily enough. And they would find Harry.

Surely her memory had to be playing her false. Karim couldn't have possibly been that devastating. That sexy. Could he?

Well, it seemed she wasn't due to have her memory jogged any time tonight at least, she told herself as she swung the little car in through the battered gates and pulled to a halt at the side of the small house. Wherever Karim was this evening, it wasn't here at Hawthorn Cottage. There was no sign of the big hulk of his car, and all the lights were off inside the house. Obviously, he had decided to go somewhere else, probably somewhere where he could have much more comfort than her small home could provide.

So was that flutter in her stomach one of relief or disappointment? She didn't dare to pursue the question any further, afraid of what it might reveal, as she pulled on the brake and switched off the engine. Not before time, she acknowledged. The silence that fell as the rattle died away made it only too clear that what she had been hearing was the death throes of the elderly car. It certainly wasn't going to take her very much further after tonight. The snow—heavy and drifting now, piling up against the walls of the cottage and blocking the narrow lane—had been the very last straw.

It was almost the last straw for her too, as she got out of the car and straight into a snowdrift that was nearly up to her thighs. Cold and wet slid into her shoes, making her shudder and she grabbed her bag, dashing towards the door. It wasn't locked, of course, she realised belatedly as she pushed it open. In her haste to be gone yesterday, to get away from Karim, she hadn't thought about locking anything after her, just to get on the road.

Another wild fall of snow whirled around her, so thick and heavy that she couldn't see more than a few feet in front of her as she stumbled into the house, deeply grateful for the warmth that even the old-fashioned central heating had thrown out while she was away. A quick glance out of the window showed that the snow had already piled inches deep on top of her car.

'Going nowhere else tonight,' she muttered, shrugging out of her coat and hanging it on a hook on the wall.

So did that mean that Karim wouldn't be able to make it to the cottage either? Did she actually have an extra night's grace?

She needed a coffee and perhaps some food before she thought about her next move, she told herself, pulling open the door into the living room. But before that she'd get the fire going to keep the house warm all through the night. She didn't know if she could rely on the heating and on several bitter nights she had actually slept downstairs on the settee with a coal fire glowing in the grate. It looked as if this was going to be one of those nights tonight.

'Good evening, Clementina,' a voice came to her from across the room. A dark, rich, male voice that she recognised in the space of a jolting, stunned heartbeat.

'What?'

Whirling in a panic, Clemmie almost flung herself towards the light switch, stabbing a finger at it in her haste to illuminate the room.

She already knew what she would see but her thoughts still reeled in shock as she came face to face with the reality. It was one thing to realise that Karim was there, in the house, silent and still, waiting for her. Quite another to confront the reality and see him sitting there, tall and proud, impossibly big, impossibly dark, ominously dangerous, his polished jet eyes fixed on her face. He was wearing another pair of jeans and a grey cashmere sweater that hugged the honed lines of his powerful chest. Simple, casual clothing but of such high quality that they looked out of place against the shabby surroundings, the worn upholstery of the armchair that seemed barely large enough to contain the lean strong frame of the powerful man who looked every bit the King's son that he was.

Surprisingly, he had a sleek tablet computer in his hands, one that he touched briefly to switch it off before letting it drop down on to his knees.

'Good evening, Clementina,' he said again, turning on a smile that was barely there and then gone again, leaving an impression of threat, of danger, without a word having to be said. 'I'm glad you made it back home.'

Was that doubt in his voice? Deliberate provocation to imply that this was the last place he expected to see her?

'I said that I would!' Clemmie protested sharply. 'And I left a note.'

Karim nodded slowly, reaching out for a piece of paper that lay on the table beside his chair. Clemmie recognised the note she had left lying on the bed and she couldn't suppress the faint shiver that skittered over her skin at the thought of what his mood must have been like when he had found it.

'"I'll be back tomorrow",' Karim read aloud, his accent making the words sound strangely alien. '"Promise".'

'I promised. And I kept my word.'

'So you did.'

And she'd surprised him there, Karim admitted. He'd been quite prepared for her to have taken off for good, turning her back on everything she had promised and leaving the situation in the most dangerous and difficult stage possible. He'd even organised contingency plans to move into action if that happened. After all, he'd had emergency plans in place before he'd even started out on the journey to England and all it would have taken would have been a couple of phone calls, and the backup team could have moved into action. He'd almost made those phone calls in the first moments after he'd lost patience with her so-called 'packing' and headed upstairs to the bedroom to bring her down, ready or not. Then he'd seen the open window, felt the icy blast of wintry air sneaking through the gaping space. He'd heard the sound of her car's engine picking up speed, heading away from the cottage. But then he'd seen the note on the bed.

'You didn't think that I would?'

'To be honest—no.'

Putting aside the tablet, he uncoiled from the uncomfortable chair, stretching cramped muscles as he did so. The tracking device he'd left on her car had worked well. When he had known that she was heading home, he had settled down to wait, listening for the sound of her car coming up to the door. Then he'd stayed silent and still so as not to have her turning and running.

'But then did you give me a reason to trust you?'

'Um…no.'

Her eyes dropped away from him as she spoke and she actually chewed at her lower lip, white teeth biting down hard on the soft pink flesh in a way that made him wince inwardly. He wanted to reach out and put his hand to her mouth, stopping the nervous gesture, but instinct held him back though his fingers twitched in anticipation of the contact. He could already feel the heat of her body, the scent of her skin reaching him and the sizzle of electricity down his nerves was like a brand on his flesh. He felt hungry, wanting in a way that was darkly carnal, just barely under control.

'I did run out on you.'

If he hadn't already met her, if he didn't know her voice, her scent and those stunning amber eyes, he might think that this was not Clementina but her double. An identical twin who had stepped in at the last minute to replace her wilder, less conventional sister. This woman was a cooler prospect altogether. Her long dark hair was caught into a shining tail that fell sleekly down her back. Her porcelain skin and golden eyes were free of any make-up—they didn't need any—and the curling black lashes that framed her gaze were impossibly thick and lush without any cosmetic enhancement.

This woman was a princess—a potential queen through and through. In spite of the fact that her clothing was once more on the far side of casual, worn denim jeans with holes at the knees and frayed hems, and an elderly dark pink jumper that had shrunk in the wash or was deliberately designed to give a disturbing glimpse of peachy skin on a tight stomach and narrow waist when she moved. She was tall and elegant. And hellishly beautiful.

But then her eyes came up fast to meet his and there was the burn of defiance in their depths.

'I did leave a note! And all I asked for was another twenty-four hours!'

The wilder Clementina was back as she tossed back her hair. He'd liked the wild Clementina better—hell, he'd loved the wild one even though he hadn't been able to show it. She'd thrown him off balance when he was already tight on edge with all that had happened. The news about his father. About Nabil. About his security chief.

'Would it have hurt so much to give me that?' she challenged.

'Not if I could have been sure that all you really wanted was those twenty-four hours.'

'I said so, didn't I? And you didn't believe me.'

'It depended on what you wanted to do with that extra day—where you planned to go. You ran away from the palace once before. How was I to know if you were setting off to some other hideaway or if you ever planned to come back.'

'I said that I would!' She turned on him a look from those brilliant eyes that was searingly scornful, even with a touch of pity threaded through it. 'It must be hellish being you—being so suspicious of everyone. Is there anyone you can trust? Anyone you can believe in?'

I believed in Razi. In spite of himself, Karim couldn't stop the thought from sliding into his mind. He had put his trust in his brother and look where that had got him. The worst failure of his life. Two deaths he hadn't been able to prevent. A whole change of life, the old one turned inside out. A new role that he had never wanted. Even a bride he had almost had to marry out of duty, if that hadn't been decided against.

'I had no reason to believe in you.'

Dark memories made his words as cold as black ice,

turning the atmosphere inside the room colder than the wintry scene outside.

'And I had no way of knowing that you were simply heading for a birthday party in Lilac Close…'

That got through to her. If he had thought that her eyes were amazing before, they were stunning now, open wide in shock and questioning bewilderment. The knowledge that he had shaken her out of her defiance gave him some satisfaction in return for the way she had escaped yesterday, leaving him with his mission unaccomplished. She had lost all colour now, her cheeks parchment-white, in contrast to the rich dark fall of her hair, those impossible eyelashes.

'How did you know?' Her voice sounded rough and raw, as if it came from a painfully dry throat.

She really didn't know who she was dealing with and the satisfaction at having wrong-footed her so completely was like a roar in his blood.

'It was easy.'

She was still staring at him as he headed for the hall, wrenching open the door. The wild fury of the snowstorm made him wince. It had been nothing like as bad as this when he had driven back to the cottage this morning. There must have been inches—more—that had fallen while he had been inside, waiting for Clementina to arrive. No wonder the reception for his computer had been spotty to say the least.

Hunching his shoulders and ducking his head, he headed out towards where her tiny elderly car was parked, its tyres already halfway deep in the drifts.

Just what was he doing now? Clemmie asked herself, as something that was not just the cold but something more, something deeper and rawer than the icy blast of the wind from outside crept round her neck and shoulders, making her shiver miserably. It was something about Karim himself. About the way he had looked at her, the ice in his eyes, the blank emotionlessness of his tone. He had been sent to fetch her and that was the one thing he was concentrated on, like a hunting dog with the scent of its prey in its nostrils. He was never going to let her go.

But how had he known where she had been? And what did that mean for Harry's safety? She could only stare in confusion as Karim dropped to his knees in the snow, reaching under the car at the front.

Jeans that were as tight a fit as that ought to be illegal. Especially over taut, muscled buttocks like this man possessed...

What *was* she thinking? Clemmie couldn't believe that the thought had flashed into her mind. She had known from a very early age that she was never going to be able to choose her own partner, her own husband. And she had also known that keeping herself respectable, not letting any scandal seep out about her was essential to her reputation. So she had never had the freedom to enjoy the company of the opposite sex like other girls, and had never even let herself think about such things. Instead, she had focused on her studies, on the books that absorbed her, the lessons with her tutor. She had never been allowed to go out to clubs or the cinema like other girls and so had missed out on chatter about boys, about fashion, even music.

Only a few months of getting to know Mary Clendon, who was just six years older than her, had changed her viewpoint, and her knowledge, on a lot of things. But she hadn't expected it to have changed to such an extent! She had never had thoughts like that about any man before.

And she had to start having them with the man who was the most unsuitable—the most inappropriate— person possible.

But Karim was getting up now, moving lithely from his position in the snow to stand upright, brushing briefly at the damp flakes still clinging to his knees before he headed back towards the cottage. The snow was whirling even more heavily, making it seem as if he was making his way through a thick white curtain, his face barely visible, his whole body just a black blur. This way, he should seem so very different. That strange, primitive, uncomfortable feeling that he seemed to spark off just by existing should be diluted by the curtain of snow.

The truth was that it was just the opposite. The contrast with the wild delicacy of the snow made him seem bigger, stronger, darker than ever, head down against the howling wind, and she felt her heart jump, skittering against her ribs as he loomed closer to the door. He came back in a rush to stride into the hall, shaking the snow from his big frame, his dark hair, like some wild animal reaching shelter from a storm.

'Here.'

He tossed something at her, something so small that it was only instinct that had her hand coming out to stop it falling to the floor.

'What?'

She stared down at the tiny metallic disk in blank confusion, not recognising it in any way.

'What is this?'

She glanced up as she spoke, meeting that darkly searching gaze head-on. But then something in his expression, the set of that sensual mouth hit home to her and she knew—she just knew. And there had been that tablet computer he had been studying when she had walked in on him in the sitting room. She had briefly glimpsed something that had looked like a map as he had put it down; a blinking cursor that marked where someone— where *she* had been.

'A tracking device!'

The words exploded from her in a blaze of indignant fury.

Did he know how this made her feel? She had been hunted as if she was a criminal and he had tracked her down. But why should he give a damn how she felt? It was why he was here; what he had come here to do.

'It's a bloody tracking device!' She tossed the disk at him, not caring that it landed on his cheek.

He didn't flinch; barely blinked and just a small brusque movement of his head sent the disk tumbling to the floor.

'And don't frown at me!' she flung at him as she saw those straight black brows twitch together in disapproval at her tone or the vehemence of her words. 'What's one little swear word in comparison to this? Or don't princesses swear in your country?'

Mistake. She knew it as she saw his expression change, his mouth tighten.

'So you remember that you are a princess,' he declared icily. 'Soon to be a queen.'

Every word was tightly enunciated, particularly the titles. He couldn't have made the atmosphere any colder if he'd tried and at that moment a freezing flurry of snow whirled in through the open door, making Clemmie shiver convulsively. With a single backward kick of one booted foot, Karim slammed the door shut and the sudden silence and stillness was unnerving. There was so little space in the small hallway and he seemed bigger, stronger than ever before. The scent of his skin coiled round her senses like some intoxicating drug, making her mouth dry, her head spin.

'And you claimed that you were a prince—Crown Prince, if I remember rightly.'

A crown prince who knew about such security devices. If he was the prince he claimed to be. A sudden rush of apprehension hit home, the room seeming to swing round her on a wave of near panic. What if he had lied all the time? If he was never who he claimed to be?

Had she done something very stupid?

He was between her and the door this time. Even if she flattened herself against the wall, there was no way he would let her squeeze past. He would grab her in an instant, hold her tight…

Shockingly, the fear that came with that thought was blended with an unholy flash of something that had no place in this situation at all. How could she feel a heated *excitement* at imagining those strong hands coming out, fastening around her arms, pulling her close…?

Suddenly she felt overdressed in the angora jumper. It really was far too warm in here. Or was that heat coming from *inside* her rather than the outside?

'I am exactly who I said I am.' The cold flicker of rich black eyelashes dismissed her question as unimportant.

'Then how do you know about such things?' Clemmie nodded towards the small disk that still lay on the floor, pushing at it with the toe of one leather boot. 'Is that the sort of hobby that crown princes have nowadays?'

'I wasn't always the Crown Prince. I had a brother. Razi.'

Had. That took away the heat in her blood, and the bleakness of his eyes made her heart twist.

'What happened?' She had to force the words out because the answer to them was so obvious.

'He died.' Cold and desolate and blunt as a hammer.

'Oh, no…' Having just begun to get to know Harry, she couldn't imagine how it would feel to lose a brother in such a shocking way. 'I'm sorry.'

It was instinctive to reach out a hand to him, but at the same time a brutal sense of self-preservation had her freezing, not having made the connection, when his iced eyes dropped to watch her and then flicked back up to her face, his expression blank and shuttered off.

'I was a security expert—in charge of defence and particularly my brother's safety.'

'But he died—so you failed him?'

Nerves made her say it. Nerves that tightened to screaming pitch when she saw the dark cloud of a scowl that distorted his stunning features, the white lines etched round his nose and mouth.

'He died in a car crash—it was his own driving that caused the accident.'

And that was all he was going to say on the subject, though she was sure there was more. There had to be more. It was hidden behind the tightly clenched jaw, the skin that was drawn too tight over powerfully carved facial bones. *Don't ask*—every line of his expression screamed it without words.

'I…' Clemmie began but Karim was looking at his watch and frowning in a very different way.

'It's time we were on our way.'

'But—I need to pack.'

'And you think I am going to fall for that again?' His scorn scoured off a much needed protective layer of her skin. 'You have your overnight bag already.' A nod of his head indicated where the bag still lay where she had dropped it as she had come through the door. 'Anything else you might need will be provided on the way. Nabil has already sent clothes for his princess. They will be on the plane, waiting for you there.'

And Clemmie could just imagine what sort of clothing that would be. Traditional costumes, formal and controlled, covering almost every inch of her body. The days of the freedom of tee shirts and jeans, her hair flying loose, were over. Already, and well before she was ready, the doors of the palace of Rhastaan were closing around her.

'I see.'

There was no point in arguing. Karim was not likely to yield on this or on any other point. She might as well beat her fists against the rigid stone of the cottage walls as beg him to give her any more time.

'Then let's get out of here.'

'You'll have to move your car first,' Karim told her. 'Mine is parked round the back and you're blocking me in. On second thoughts…' He reached for the car key that she had tossed on to the small table in the hall. 'I'll drive—and don't even think about running off.'

'I wouldn't! I only went…' Her voice died away. Did he know why she had gone or just where she had gone? 'I only asked for twenty-four hours—and I said I'd be back. I am back and I'm not planning on running off. You have to believe me.'

Strangely, he did, Karim admitted—today, at least.

Yesterday he'd had a very different opinion of her. But yesterday he'd been angry, tense, too much to think of and collecting Nabil's errant bride being one more thing he didn't want on his shoulders. His father's heart problems and the suspicion that they had been brought on by the stress of the loss of his eldest son and heir had been the last straw. He couldn't get away from the fact that if he had refused to give in to Razi's demand that he have no security detail, his brother might still be here.

Today he felt differently. And it wasn't just because she had come back when she'd said. This new, calmer, dignified Clementina was a very different prospect from the wild, defiant creature who had opened the door to him yesterday and had sneaked out of the house at the first opportunity.

But some instinct had made him give her the twenty-four hours she had asked for. The tracking device had shown that she was at Lilac Close. A few discreet enquiries had revealed that she was friends with the family who lived there. Who were holding a birthday party for their young son. He'd decided to give her the chance and wait.

He was surprisingly glad that he had. And when the door had opened and she'd walked in something had changed inside him. Something unexpected and unsettling. Something he didn't want to take out and face. Not when he had to get this mission completed and one princess delivered to her prospective bridegroom, putting his father's mind at rest on this at least.

He'd already been delayed twenty-four hours too long. It was time they were on the road and heading out of here.

There was no chance of that, Karim realised only a very short time later. He'd already had doubts when he went outside again. Yet more snow had piled up around

Clementina's car. The wheels were half hidden under the drifting snow, the path to the road had been obliterated, and the garden was a white-out. The vehicle was going to be very little use in these conditions. It was lucky he had his four-wheel drive in the yard at the back of the house. If he could only get it on to the road.

But the little car's engine refused to start. Every time he turned the key in the ignition there was a dreadful grating, rasping noise that sounded as if the elderly car was breathing its last. It choked and spluttered—and died with a shudder. One that made him curse and slam his hands down on the steering wheel in exasperation.

'Is there a problem?' Clementina had come out of the house and was leaning down to the window, frowning in concern.

'You could say that.' Once more he tried turning the key. There wasn't even a groan from the engine. 'This car isn't going anywhere today—tonight,' he amended, glaring up at the darkening sky.

'Perhaps if I steered and you pushed...'

'We could try.'

'OK then.' She made a move to hurry out of the way of the opening car door. 'Let me into the driver's seat and I'll... Oh!'

The sentence broke off on a sharp cry of distress as she stepped on a patch of ice hidden under the snow. With a yelp, she fought to stay upright, one leg going one way, the other heading in the opposite direction. Her foot twisted under her, throwing her completely off balance and she fell headlong, landing heavily in a deep snowdrift.

CHAPTER FOUR

'KARIM!'

Her cry of distress was too high, too shocked, to be anything but genuine, setting his nerves on edge and pushing him out of the car as fast as his reflexes would allow.

'Clementina…'

She was struggling to get up, slipped a little and then collapsed again on a small moan.

'What hurts?' Because it was obvious that something did.

'My ankle…'

She was biting her lip hard and only by diverting his attention to the right ankle she had indicated with a wave did he stop himself from pressing his fingers against her mouth to stop the damaging action.

'I fell over on it—twisted it…'

There was nothing to see. Nothing, that was, except the temptation of soft pale flesh, delicate bones, the base of a long slender leg… He ran his hands over the skin of her ankle, pressed gently. Fought against the burn of response that flashed up his nerves as he did so.

'Can you stand?'

He knew his tone was rough and abrupt; didn't need

the reproachful look she cast at him. Reproach that melted into defiance as her chin came up and her mouth firmed.

'I can try.'

Stubbornly, she ignored the hand he held out to her, relying instead on supporting herself on the car's bumper as she hauled herself up. Then, just as she stood upright, she gave another gasping cry as she tried to put her weight on the injured limb.

'OK…'

He caught her before she fell, swung her off the ground and up into his arms.

'Let's get you inside.'

He sensed her rebellion, the tensing of her body, but then, clearly recognising that she wasn't going to manage this on her own, she made herself relax against him. He was grateful for the need to watch his step on the icy path, the fight against the whirling snow as he hurried inside. It distracted him from the feel of her, warm and soft against him. The perfume of her skin rose up, tantalising his senses, and the softness of her hair was like silk against his cheek.

Karim didn't know if he was relieved or sorry when he made it inside the house, shouldering his way along the narrow hall and into the living room. He laid her down on the settee, not caring if the haste of his movements, the abruptness of his actions made it seem as if he was glad to be relieved of the burden of her weight. He *was* relieved, but not because her weight was too much for him to carry. He'd managed much heavier weights over much longer distances before now. But nothing he'd ever carried before had made his heart beat so fast, his breath tangle in his throat so that he was breathing as hard as if he'd run a marathon.

'I'll take your boot off.'

It was a good thing that there wasn't a visible pulse in her ankle, Clemmie reflected as she watched Karim's dark silky head bend over her foot, unlacing and easing the boot from her foot. If there was then he would be sure to see the effect his closeness was having on her, the way that her heartbeat responded to the touch of his hands, the warmth of his breath on her skin. It made her insides twist, her nerves tangle.

This was the first time that she'd seen all that strength and power used in a very different way. A gentle, caring, helpful way. In the moment that he'd picked her up she had felt as if a shield had come round her, blocking off the cold blast of the snowstorm, protecting her from it. And being held against the warmth and strength of his chest had felt like being enclosed in the strongest, most wonderful hug ever, with the heavy regular beat of his heart just under her cheek.

Then she had felt nothing but warmth, but now she felt alternately burningly hot and then shiveringly cold, as if she was in the grip of some delirious fever. The heat in her blood was raw and primitive, a visceral feeling that clawed at her, fraying away her sense of self, leaving her feeling out of control and wildly adrift. She had never felt this way before and it shocked and disturbed her, making her pull away from Karim's grip as she sat up hastily, wanting to escape from it.

'I'll do that,' she snapped, hiding her real feelings behind a mask of indignation.

She wanted to move as far from Karim as possible, but in the same moment that she twisted away she felt surprisingly lost and bereft, needing the warm protection of his body—needing so much more.

'I can manage…'

Unfastening the boot, pulling it from her foot was no problem at all but she made herself focus on it as if it was a struggle, rather than face the real struggle that was going on inside her. Her heart was thudding unevenly, her breath ragged and uneven.

'Are you all right?'

He'd heard the way she was breathing, put the wrong sort of interpretation on it. But that was the way she wanted him to interpret it, wasn't it?

'I'm fine.'

Even in her own ears it didn't sound convincing, no matter how emphatic she made it, so she put on a hiss of discomfort as she pulled the boot from her foot and tossed it to the floor.

'I might have sprained this—it's swollen.'

No, that had been a mistake, as it brought him back to her, those long, square-tipped fingers touching her ankle lightly, testing, stroking…

More! The word burned inside her head and she almost choked trying to swallow it down. *I want more than this.*

'I think…'

Another mistake. Just speaking had brought his head up, made his gaze lock with hers. She could see the black thickness of his lashes in absurd detail, find a tiny reflected replica of herself in the depths of those amazing eyes. His skin smelt of musk and lemon, making her head spin as she inhaled when she breathed.

'You think?' Something had put that note of huskiness into his voice. The fullness of his mouth had a faint sheen where he had moistened it lightly with his tongue. Had he felt as dry-throated, found it as hard to swallow as she had?

'Perhaps something cold would help ease it—reduce the swelling?'

'Good idea.' He pushed himself upright with a speed and satisfaction that scraped her tight nerves painfully raw. 'Then we might actually be able to get on the road—get out of here.'

Did he have to make it so plain that all that mattered to him was their getting on their way? She must have been totally deluding herself thinking that he might actually respond to her as she was reacting to him. Daft idea. Stupid—crazy idea! Just what would a man like Karim—like Crown Prince Karim Al Khalifa—find of any interest in someone like her? Someone in tatty jeans and a sweater, her hair unstyled and usually just left to fall free. Someone who was happier with books and paintings than the clubs and bars her friends were fascinated by.

Someone who must wear her naiveté and ignorance where the opposite sex was concerned like a brand on her forehead. And show it in every unguarded move, every artless look. A man like Karim would be seen with sophisticated glamorous women. He would be like Nabil who, even though he was so much younger, had already been spotted with beautiful models or actresses. He had the freedom to play the field. To sow his wild oats before tying himself down to the arranged marriage that had been planned for them both.

'Peas,' she said abruptly, her uncomfortable thoughts not giving her room to think of anything extra to make it less stark, less brusque. 'Freezer...'

That was no better but at least she waved her hand in the direction of the kitchen. And at least he followed her vague gesture, moving away so that she had time to catch her breath, fight to bring her heart rate under control.

'Wrapping a bag of frozen peas around it might work.' He didn't need the explanation, was already opening the freezer door and rummaging through the bags and containers in there.

'If I have any peas...'

A sudden thought struck her and she couldn't control her response, unable to hold back the giggle that bubbled up in her chest.

'What is it?'

He didn't sound as irritable as before. In fact there was actually a softening warmth in his tone. Or was she just deceiving herself, wanting to hear it?

'What are you laughing about?'

'I can't believe that we are struggling to find a packet of frozen peas when there is all that ice and snow outside! Can't you just fill a plastic bag with the stuff and wrap that around my ankle?'

'It might work—but—ah!' He pounced on something inside the freezer. 'Not peas—but I'm sure sweetcorn will have exactly the same effect. You have so little food in the freezer,' he said as he came back to crouch down by the settee again. 'Barely enough to feed a bird.'

'I was running it all down, getting ready to move away from here—to Rhastaan— Ouch!'

He had dumped the frozen bag on her ankle with a surprising lack of finesse, nothing like the powerful and contained grace of movement he had showed up to now.

'Did that hurt?'

Frantically, Clemmie shook her head, afraid that he would replace the chill of the frozen vegetables with that disturbing and dangerous warmth of his hands, the unsettling feel of his touch.

'No—just the cold! It was a shock. But I'm sure it will help—'

'It had better. We need to get out of here.'

It was as if the few moments it had taken him to hunt through the freezer had pushed the ice into his soul and turned it hard and glacial all over again. But more likely the truth was that she had been letting her imagination run away with her when she had thought she'd heard that unexpected streak of warmth that had softened his tone.

'You're not still thinking of leaving tonight? You're mad! Have you ever tried driving in conditions like this?'

'I have lived—and driven—in Europe before.'

But not in a snowstorm like the one raging outside, Karim had to admit to himself. Under normal circumstances, he would stay right where he was. But these were not normal circumstances. There was nothing normal about the situation he had been put in, first by his father, then Nabil—and now Clementina.

And there was nothing normal about his reaction to her. The soul-twisting, gut-wrenching, brutally carnal hunger this woman woke in him.

Hell and damnation!

Karim pushed himself to his feet and swung away from watching her as she clamped the bag of frozen sweetcorn around her ankle. He couldn't bear to see the way the colour had left her cheeks and then unexpectedly flooded right back into them again. The way she was still worrying at the softness of her lip and, worst of all, the unexpected vulnerability in her eyes. Each one of those responses would twist at his gut. Taken together, they were lethal to his self-control.

Stupid, stupid, stupid! Karim told himself as he headed for the door. He should know better—he did know better.

But knowing and convincing himself that this was not going to happen was getting harder with each thundering beat that made his pulse thud at his temples.

He hadn't had a woman in a long time. Too long. Another thing that was part of the mess that his life had become in the past six months. The upside down and inside out version of the existence he had once had. And that was nothing like it would ever be again.

Perhaps the time spent outside, trying to get the car going again would give him a much-needed dose of reality. Certainly, the cold of the wind and snow should have the effect of an icy shower to cool the heat of his blood. Permanently, he hoped. When he had looked into Clementina's eyes and seen the bruised pansy darkness there, the heat that had flooded his senses had been a form of madness that had sent his brain into meltdown.

It had been strong enough to make him forget for a moment just who she was, and why he was here. It had made him realise just how much he had pushed aside his own needs to deal with other things.

And those needs had now come rushing back in the form of the one woman who was the last person on earth he should feel those things for.

The snow whirled wildly into his face as he opened the door, making him grimace, bring up his hands against the onslaught. He could barely see through the white curtain but he had no intention of turning back. The exercise and the fight against the cold were the only possible antidote he could think of to the frustration that was burning up inside him.

How much longer was he going to be?

Clemmie could not fight against the restlessness that had assailed her since Karim had disappeared out of the door and let it slam behind him. She needed to know what was happening, when they might get on the road. The evening had started to gather in, filling the room with darkness, but when she had tried to get up to switch on more lights, the pain in her ankle had had her sinking back on to the settee with a cry of distress. But if things got any worse, she was going to have to try again. The cold was beginning to fill the air too and she was starting to feel uncomfortably chilled just sitting here.

She was just about to try to push herself to her feet again when the front door banged open and Karim appeared in the hallway. A Karim who looked more like a moving snowman than anything human, his jacket was so piled up with snow and his hair plastered against the strong bones of his skull by the damp.

'At last!' she said.

She pushed herself up in her seat as he stood on the doormat, stamping his feet to clear them of the clinging snow.

'Are we on our way?'

It was inevitable they must be. That was what he had come for—to collect her and take her back to Rhastaan. She wouldn't—couldn't let the painful clenching of her stomach make her think of how it felt to be starting out on this journey, heading for the life she hadn't chosen but she had known must come to be hers. And leaving behind the only true member of her family she had ever known. Her father didn't count. He had only seen her as a pawn in his political manoeuvrings and her mother had walked out on her without a glance back.

'Shall I get my coat?'

If her voice went up and down unnaturally then surely he would think it was because she was struggling to get to her feet. Even she didn't understand the sudden change in her heartbeat, the skittering of her pulse as she took in the stark contrast between the white of the snow and the dark power of the rest of Karim's body, the heavy silhouette of his frame in the doorway, illuminated by the one hanging light.

'No.'

It was stark and cold, biting as harshly as the wind that sneaked down the hall, taking even more of the minimal warmth from the room so that she shivered in more than physical response. What had happened to the man who had laughed with her over the pack of frozen sweetcorn?

'But I thought...'

'Don't think,' Karim snarled.

He pulled off the snow-laden jacket, tossed it aside, stamping his feet again with a sound that echoed ominously in the silence.

'And don't say another word—not unless you can come up with some clever idea as to how we can get the heap of scrap you call a car to move more than a metre or two.'

'It's not a heap of scrap!' Clemmie flared, coming to the defence of her sweet little car. It might be old, it might be a bit battered, but it was hers and it had spelled freedom and escape when she had needed it most. 'We can't all drive the latest luxury four-wheel...'

'You could if you wanted to—' Karim cut in sharply, bringing her to an abrupt halt '—if you'd stayed with your father or in Rhastaan. As Nabil's queen...'

If Nabil would even let her drive, Clemmie told herself. Young as he was, he was traditionalist enough to insist on his wife staying inside, emerging only with an escort, or with Nabil himself. Women in Rhastaan had not been allowed to drive during his father's reign. So would that be permitted now?

'Now I wonder why—' she began, only to break off as a worrying, disturbing thought hit home like a blow. 'My car won't move?'

'Not an inch, not in these conditions. And as my car is trapped in the yard behind it, then we're stuck. Unless I can get a garage truck out—do you have a number?'

He gestured towards the old-fashioned phone on the hall table. Clemmie's heart sank several degrees lower.

'That's not going to help. I had it cut off as part of my preparations to leave. I've been relying on my mobile, even though the reception's unreliable.'

She pulled her phone out her pocket, checked it, then held it out to him, her face spelling out her disappointment.

'Nothing. Yours? Or your tablet? It was working when I arrived.'

One touch of his thumb to the phone told the same story. Not a single bar to indicate any connection. And it was the same with his computer.

'The Internet's down too—everything. This storm has really damaged everything. So, for the foreseeable future, we're imprisoned here until something changes.'

She wished he hadn't used that word 'imprisoned'. It sounded too stark, too dangerous, too scary to face in a moment like this, isolated in this tiny cottage with a man as dark and ruthlessly determined as Karim Al Khalifa.

'Then what…' she began, wondering just how things could get any worse.

But, even as she spoke, the single light illuminating the hall flickered, crackled loudly and then went out, leaving them in total darkness.

'Karim!'

His name was a cry of shock and near panic, the instinct to turn to him coming from somewhere deep and unexpectedly primitive. The blackness around her was thick and almost impenetrable, the only hint of any light coming from the reflected whiteness of the snow beyond the window. She struggled up from her seat on the sofa, the breath hissing in through her teeth as she put her weight on her bruised ankle.

'I'm here.'

Something flared in the darkness. He was using the phone as a torch, the screen lighting the room for a moment. It shone straight up into his face, showing it dark and shuttered, strangely shadowed in the glow, but Clemmie felt that she had never been so pleased to see anyone in her life. The cottage that had previously been safety and home to her now felt like something else entirely. The real world had invaded her sanctuary. It was Karim who had brought that reality, that world in with him, and yet it was Karim that she felt she could turn to. She was glad that he was here. Only one day earlier he had invaded her life, shocking and disturbing her, and yet without him she would have felt lost and adrift on a sea as wild as the storm raging outside.

Karim seemed almost like part of that storm. Harsh and forceful as the weather, like some untamed creature that had come in from the night, his power and presence filled the small house. It was strange that the golden tones of his skin, his name and his accent all came from a land of heat and sun, but here, in the dark and wildness of the icy snow, he still had a power that seemed at one with the elements. This was her home and he was the intruder, but in the darkness and the cold she was grateful for the strength of his very physical company.

'The power's gone…' Stupid and weak as it sounded, it was all she could manage. 'Are you sure we're stuck here for the night?'

'Certain.'

He'd been flicking switches, checking plugs, to make sure that it was not just the bulb or the wiring in the hall and now he was nodding grimly, mouth clamped tight over the anger he clearly would not allow himself to express.

'Nothing, damn it. Do you have a torch? Candles? I need to conserve the power on my phone.'

'Candles in the cupboard under the sink. My torch is in the car.'

She'd thought she might need it on the journey to visit Harry, not once she was back safe in her own home. It was a struggle to just stand there and watch him as he groped his way to the kitchen, hunted in the cupboard. Rattled by all that had happened, and with her twisted ankle still nagging at her painfully, she was so tempted to move to his side, fling her arms around him…feel his strength close around her as it had done when he had picked her up from the snow outside. What stopped her was an instinctive feeling that that would be overstepping an invisible line, risking…

Risking what? A stunningly physical response or, more likely, an immediate rejection—or, even worse, a careful, condescending putting her away from him so that he could get on with the practical matter that he was focused on. She couldn't bear the humiliation of that and it was more than enough to hold her where she was in spite of the yearning that still twisted in her stomach.

A scratching sound of match on box from the kitchen seemed unnaturally loud in the silence. There was a small flare, and the flickering flame of the candle added a tiny light to the darkness.

'There are no holders...'

'No, but we could stick them on saucers,' Clemmie told him, making her way gingerly into the kitchen.

Luckily the cupboard containing the plates and cups was at the other end of the kitchen so, even feeling her way with her hands, she was in no danger of touching him. But she could still see that stunning face in the flickering candle flame, could scent his skin and his hair, drying slowly after the exposure to the snow. She could even see the tiny flecks of the white flakes that decked his long lashes like miniature diamonds and her mouth itched to kiss them away, licking the moisture from his lids with her tongue.

And where had that thought come from? Shock at the way her mind was working had her banging the saucers down on the kitchen worktop with a distinct crash. She had never felt like this with anyone before. And not just because she had tried to keep her mind off such things. She had just never felt this way ever.

'Careful!' Karim's reproof was low and strangely touched with warmth. It was as if he knew only too well what was going through her mind and that thought made her hand shake as she reached for another of the candles.

'Careful yourself—they're my saucers—my candles...'

To her horror she had mistimed the reach, her fingers grabbing at the candle Karim held rather than the spare unlit ones in his other hand. In the same moment the awkward movement twisted at her sore ankle again, making her overbalance and tumble headlong towards him.

'*Careful!*'

It was so very different this time. Every trace of that warmth, the light amusement had faded from the single word and the edge on his tone sent shivers down her spine. Shivers that combined with the shock of electricity where her fingers had closed over the hand that held the candle. It was impossible not to think of the shape she held, long and hard, and capable of such heat.

She had one moment to try to recover, one moment of looking up straight into his eyes and seeing the darkness there that was more than the shadows surrounding them, the burn of something that was more than the reflection of the flame he held between them. But then, as she almost overbalanced, he reacted swiftly, dropping the candle into the sink so that she didn't fall dangerously close to it but instead stumbled right into his arms.

In the darkness again, it was more than she had anticipated. More than she could ever have expected. Her face was up against his chest, pressed into the softness of the cashmere, crushed against the hardness of collarbone and ribcage, inhaling the scent of his skin, feeling the heat and the muscles in his throat against her brow. She heard him draw in a sharp breath, sensed him swallow hard, wished she could do the same to ease the choking dryness in her own mouth.

She felt his hands come out to hold her, stop her from falling, and her breath caught in her throat as the heat of those hard palms reached her through her clothing, searing the skin on her thighs, her waist. She could have sworn that his hands lingered, curling closer, holding her against him so that she couldn't break free even if she'd wanted to. But breaking free was the last thing on her mind. Her heart had taken off at an alarming rate, blood thundering in her ears. But Karim's pulse rate was as cool and controlled as if he had simply just caught hold of the handle of a broom or mop—rather than a living breathing woman.

And yet…

'Shall we try again?'

There was a definite sardonic edge to the question, an almost brutal stiffness in the way he caught her arms and straightened her up, moving her away from him as if he suddenly felt that her touch would contaminate him. She could sense no reluctance to let her go, catch no sense of regret in that calmly indifferent voice. But just for a second she had been crushed up against him and even as the heat of her own response had flooded through her she had known that he had to be feeling something too. There was no denying the hard and heated evidence of his body crammed against hers; the evidence of a carnal hunger that not even a virgin with as little experience of men as she had could possibly mistake in any way. It could have—should have—frightened her but instead it sent a secret, stinging thrill running through her.

'Karim…'

Protest, encouragement or question? She didn't know, didn't care. Her head was swimming, every cell in her body seemed to be on fire at just the thought that a man like this—this man—could want her in that way. She ached and needed in a way she'd never thought possible, heat and moisture waking deep inside. And she hoped…

But already he was bending, picking up the candle. He turned to pull the saucers towards him, dismissing her from his thoughts, before reaching again for the box of matches. It was business as usual, and he was cold and distant again. So withdrawn that she began to believe she had imagined any other reaction. Was she really so desperate, so like some schoolgirl in the middle of her first heavy crush, that she was allowing herself to dream that the most devastating man she had ever met would want her, of all people?

As the light from the candles flooded into the darkness it seemed as if it was followed by a shiver of reality that reproached her for fooling herself. In the same moment that the flame illuminated some sections of the room, it also darkened and deepened the shadows of others, making them bleak and impenetrable as Karim's shuttered face. And with it came an awareness of the way that the atmosphere in the room had changed, physically as well as mentally.

CHAPTER FIVE

'The…the electricity going out means that the heating has gone off too,' she managed, needing to say something to break the silence that had tightened round her. 'This house is going to get really cold very fast.'

It was already starting to chill rapidly in a way for which even Karim's glacial stare couldn't take the blame. The eerie sound of the wind howling around outside, rattling the elderly windows in their ill-fitting frames, added to the uncomfortable atmosphere.

'You have a fire.' Karim nodded towards the open grate.

'If it will light!' Clemmie acknowledged, knowing from bitter experience how difficult that could be. 'I've spent I don't know how many hours fighting with the damn thing in the past.'

'It will light.'

Karim's statement was resolute, adamant. The fire would do as it was told. It would light; it had no choice.

And it did light, of course. With an ease that made a mockery of all the times she had battled with the old-fashioned grate, he soon had strong flames catching on the wood he'd laid as kindling, licking around the coal.

The crackling sound it made, the sparks that flew up the chimney promised that warmth would soon follow.

Which, of course, it did. Karim was in charge and nothing dared defy him. And Clemmie had to admit that she was more than thankful to see the golden glow fill the grate, feel the heat reaching out to touch skin that was now chilled through as the darkness closed in around them, the candles providing only a minimum of light. They would need to ration them if the electricity stayed off much longer. The half dozen or so she had in the cupboard would barely last the night. She didn't want to admit to herself that some of the ice that seemed to have filled her veins had come from the realisation of just what a fool she had been. Imagining that Karim of all people could actually find her attractive—could want her!

The way he had immediately turned his attention to the task in hand, clearly forgetting all about her and any connection she might have imagined they'd made, told her in no uncertain terms that that fantasy had been all hers. And a fantasy was what it was.

'Do you have any food for this evening?'

Karim kept his eyes focused on the fire as he spoke. It had been bad enough in the dark with her. The half-light of the candles and the fire was too alluring where it played over the warm curves of Clementina's body, put an extra spark into the depth of her eyes. Being blind accentuated all your other senses and, though he hadn't actually been blind, being lost in the complete darkness had had the same effect.

He had felt the warmth of her skin, inhaled the subtle floral and spice scent of her perfume. A perfume that was threaded through with the intensely personal aroma of the feminine body that had come so close to his. He had felt the warmth of her skin through the denim of her jeans when his hands lingered, longing, tempted, around the curve of her hips, the indentation of her waist. And in the deep silence, all outside muffled by the heavy coating of snow that had fallen, he could hear the soft sound of her breathing, knew the moment when it caught in her throat and then broke again in a faint hiccup of response to his touch.

Fool! Bloody stupid fool!

He rammed the poker in amongst the hot coals, feeling that he knew exactly how they must feel. He had arrived at the cottage—was it less than forty-eight hours before?—thinking that all he had to do was to get the woman he had been sent to collect into his car, drive her to the airport, and deliver her to her prospective bridegroom. But from the moment he had seen Clementina Savanevski he had known he was in trouble.

How badly in trouble he hadn't realised quite then.

Suddenly his life and the plan he had for it had been turned on its head. Clementina had been nothing like he had expected and he had never anticipated the force of his own response to her. She had already delayed their departure by her disappearing act—and now this!

'That's the bad news.'

Her voice came from behind him and he knew he should turn to face her. But for now he wanted to stay turned away, to focus his attention on the fire before him, to tell himself that the heat of the flames was what was burning him up inside. It had nothing to do with anything else.

Nothing.

'What's the bad news?'

No, dammit, the fire was settled and going fine. He

was going to look like all sorts of a fool if he didn't turn. So much so that she would suspect there was something up and he didn't want her thinking any such thing. He had made it seem as if the practicalities—candles, light, warmth—were all that mattered to him. They were all that should matter to him. And he didn't want to let any suspicion of anything else slide into her mind.

'What's the bad news?' he demanded again as he swung round.

She was standing behind the old shabby settee, holding on to the back in a way that suddenly made him remember her injured ankle and curse himself for forgetting. Without that they might still have been on their way out of here, but she'd fallen and he'd had to bring her inside. Another delay to add to the ones that had ruined every last detail of the plans he'd had to fulfil his promise to his father and then get on with his own life while he could.

Cursing silently, he felt for the phone that he had pushed into the back pocket of his jeans and checked it again. The screen told him all he needed to know. There wasn't a hint of reception. Not a single bar to show even the hope of any call getting through. They were well and truly trapped. As he acknowledged the thought the whirling wind of the storm outside built up in power and ferocity to emphasise the point.

'The food.'

She'd noticed his abstraction and was frowning faintly.

'There might be some bits and pieces in the fridge— but I won't be able to do much with them. The cooker is electric…'

A wave of her hand indicated the elderly and inadequately fitted kitchen.

'So that's gone—so has the kettle. I can offer you a sandwich…'

'I'll make it.'

Karim was already moving towards the kitchen. Did he have to make it so obvious he was impatient and anxious to be away from her? Clemmie wondered. If he had checked his phone once, he'd checked it a hundred times and he had only given up on moving her car when the storm had driven him inside.

'I'll do it!' she protested, pushing him aside as she hobbled into the other room. 'Small and tatty as it is, this is my house! You can't come in here and throw your weight around just because you're Crown Prince of somewhere…'

'I was thinking of your ankle.' It was a mocking drawl, one that made her stiffen her back in defiance. 'Can you manage to stand on it?'

'I'm fine.'

She would do it or die in the attempt, Clemmie told herself, grabbing the remains of a loaf from the bread bin and slamming it down on to the worktop. She was already regretting moving much at all, with her ankle aching and protesting fiercely when she put her weight on it. She opened the fridge door awkwardly and peered in, balancing precariously on her sound leg.

'Cheese? Salad?'

The exclamation of annoyance from behind her should have warned her, but she was so determined on not looking at him that she missed it completely. All she knew was that she was suddenly grabbed from behind, snatched up into the air and carried forcibly back into the sitting room. There Karim dumped her unceremoniously on to the settee and pushed her back into the cushions with a firm hand when she struggled to get up again.

'Stay there,' he said in the sort of voice he might use to control a dog. One he expected to be obeyed.

Clemmie decided against fighting him over this. He'd been right about her ankle, though it galled her to have to admit it, and the warmth of the fire was welcome after the sneaking chill of the kitchen. She huddled closer to the grate and hugged a cushion tightly for comfort. It did nothing to wipe away the burn of Karim's touch, ease the uneven lurch of her heart. The scent of his skin still lingered on her sleeve where he had held her and, believing he was occupied with the food, she couldn't resist the primal urge to rub her cheek against it, inhaling deeply.

'Food… Such as it is.'

She jumped like a startled cat as a plate came over the back of the settee, pushed almost into her face. Had he seen anything? Had he caught the betraying reaction she'd just given in to? With the scent of his hands still in her nostrils she felt the nerves in her body spring into painful pins and needles life as Karim came close to the fire. Would he sit beside her on the sofa? She didn't know if she could bear it, cope with it, if he did. But in the same heartbeat she wanted it; longed for it with a burn that scorched her nerves.

So it was impossible to snatch back the sigh that escaped her when Karim took the only other seat in the room, pulling the battered brown armchair up to the fire as he sat down with his own sandwich on a plate. She saw that the sound had caught his attention, watched that warning frown appear between his dark brows, and nerved herself for the inevitable sarcastic comment.

Surprisingly it didn't come.

'Why do you live here? Like this,' Karim demanded instead.

The way he looked round the room, dark eyes assessing, made her grit her teeth. She knew the cottage was shabby. But she liked it that way. It was the way that Nan had left it when she'd died and it brought back such wonderful happy memories of those brief childhood visits.

'I'm sorry if it's not the sort of palace that you are used to.'

'Nor the sort of palace *you* are used to,' Karim parried. 'And very definitely not the sort of place you will be living in from now on.'

Don't remind me! Did he really think that would be the sort of thing that would make her think differently about this cottage? That she would actually prefer the marble palace of Rhastaan where her life had been signed away as a child and from which she could never hope to escape?

'But this place is my own! All mine and no one else's.'

And until Karim's arrival, no one from Markhazad or any of the surrounding desert kingdoms had known anything about it. He had invaded her privacy, stalking into her home like some dark, arrogant wild cat, taking with him her last traces of seclusion and solitude. From now on her life would not be her own. She would live in the public eye if she ever set foot outside the palace. And inside… Her mind skittered away from considering the prospect of life with the husband who had been chosen for her, the emptiness of a political marriage from which she had no escape.

If he had looked like Karim, though…

'Yours?' Karim queried.

She really had his attention now. That probing gaze,

dark with disbelief, was fixed on her face, and a frown had snapped his black brows together.

'My grandmother lived here, and I visited sometimes when I was a child. She left me the cottage in her will—and—well, there didn't seem much point in changing it seeing as I was only here for such a short time and...'

She had foolishly taken a small bite of her sandwich and now her throat closed sharply over the bread so that she almost choked. She grabbed at the glass of water, all they had to drink, and swigged it desperately, hoping that he would miss the tears in her eyes or at least take them for the result of her coughing fit rather than a reaction to the cruel combination of past memories and the prospect of the future that had assailed her. Karim didn't move an inch, didn't even blink, his own sandwich part raised from his plate but frozen in mid-air. She could feel the burn of his searing stare, those dark eyes seeming to strip away a defensive layer of skin and leaving her raw and vulnerable underneath.

'Two day-old bread!' she managed by way of an explanation, waving her own sandwich in front of her face in the hope of distracting him. 'Too dry.'

It was too, she realised with a grimace as she made herself force another mouthful down. She had been expecting to move on from the cottage, so her supplies of food had been deliberately run down.

'So you were planning on going back?' He'd picked up on what she had been about to say without her having to complete the sentence.

That brought her head back, her chin coming up in defiance as she blinked the betraying tears away from her eyes in order to be able to face him. In the firelight, shadows flickered and danced across his rough-carved face, making it impossible to read what thoughts the black ice of his eyes really held deep inside them.

'Don't sound so surprised. Of course I was going back.' The prospect of what might happen if she hadn't made her shudder inwardly. 'In fact there was no need for your father to send you—or anyone else to come and fetch me.'

Oh, but there was. Karim prayed that his reaction didn't show on his face. He had no wish to have her panicking and making things so much worse. If they could get any worse.

His appetite vanishing in the blink of an eye, he tossed his sandwich down on to his plate and slammed it on to the small coffee table. He was supposed to be out of here now, and well on his way back to Rhastaan. In fact they should have been there already, landing at the airport where Nabil's security men would be waiting to take over. He would be free of his duty, of the promises that had been made, free of the burden of responsibility for Clementina, and on his way back to his own life.

Except that the changes in that life meant that he would never again be really free. No longer the 'spare' to Razi's heir, with the extra degrees of independence that had brought, he was now learning what it meant to be the future Sheikh of Markhazad. Belatedly, he felt he had begun to understand just why a sense of rebelliousness, of restlessness had driven his brother. He also had to try to be both sons to his father, who had felt the loss of his heir so terribly.

But to think of Clementina as a burden grated against something deep inside. Her position and the promises his father had made, the peace treaties that were at risk now, were what made this situation so difficult. Without them, being with this beautiful woman, whose face was lit by the flames in the hearth, putting a glow into her eyes, tinting her skin with gold, would be no burden at all.

Hell, no!

Ferociously he slammed a door shut in his mind, cutting out the dangerous thoughts. But it was too late. Already his senses had responded, his blood flooding with a heat that had nothing to do with the burning coals that were only making the smallest impact on the encroaching cold. His gaze fixed on the softness of her lips, gilded by the light, so full, so soft that his own mouth hungered to take them, to plunder their sweetness, feel them give way under his, yield to the invasion of his tongue. He wanted to tangle his hands in the fall of her hair, inhale the intimate scent of her body, feel the softness of her breasts against him as he had when he'd carried her into the house after her fall in the snow.

Damnation, he wanted more than that. He wanted her on her back on this rug right in front of the fire. He wanted her under him, holding him, her body arching up to meet his, pressing herself closer…

No.

Grabbing his glass of water, he downed the entire contents in a series of harsh, powerful gulps that did nothing to douse the fires inside him. His body ached, the hardness between his legs making it impossible to sit comfortably, so that he pushed himself to his feet and paced around the room, finding a new frustration in the impossibly small space that confined him. What he needed was a brutal workout, a punishing run for miles until he was exhausted, or an ice-cold shower to subdue his demanding libido.

All of which were impossible for him, even the cold

shower. Unless he went outside into the snowstorm, of course. And he could just imagine Clementina's reaction if he did any such thing.

And, the way he was feeling, he doubted that even jumping into one of the snowdrifts would do anything to cool the heat that had been building up inside him ever since he had first met Clementina.

She was watching him now, her eyes wide with confusion and bewilderment, and who could blame her? He was acting like a captured wolf, trapped in too small a cage. He had to get a grip and distract himself from the hunger that was eating at him.

Talking. That might do it. Talk about anything—anything but sex. Think about anything but sex. And then when he was out of here he would find the nearest, most willing woman and lose himself in her. It might take more than one but at least he could have fun trying.

Now, what had they been talking about? The cottage and the fact that she had come here—running away from her duty.

'So why didn't you tell anyone where you were—and that you'd be back?'

It was the last thing Clementina had been expecting. She had been sure that he had something else on his mind, something that had brought that black scowl to his face, tightened the muscles in his long body until they made him stand as if he was ready for a fight.

'Leave another note like the one I left you?'

Broad shoulders shrugged off her challenge, her shaky defiance seeming to bounce off those taut muscles.

'I doubt very much that I'd have been believed. And then...'

But no, that was going too far. He already knew where

she had been last night. The address was obviously filed away in some database on his computer, along with the trail that the tracking device had followed to Mary's house. If she let anyone suspect that Harry existed, that he had been adopted after her mother's unexpected death, then it would be the easiest thing to hunt down 3 Lilac Close and...

Following his example, she tossed the bread and cheese down on to her plate and pushed it aside, unable to think of eating any more. What she was doing would protect Harry—and Mary and Arthur. It would give them the future that she couldn't hope for herself. She had signed the cottage away to the Clendons and she could only hope that they, and especially Harry, would love it as much as she had.

'Yet you left me a note—and expected it to be believed.'

And even now she was still asking herself why. Not why she had left it. That had been the only honourable thing she could do. She couldn't just have taken off out of here without leaving some communication that said she was coming back, that the future that was all mapped out for her was one she accepted—she had to accept.

But she didn't quite know why she had thought that it mattered particularly to leave it for *him*—and that he would believe she had meant it.

'But you didn't really believe me—did you?' she challenged. 'You didn't need to, for one thing—you had that tracking device on my car. You could have come and picked me up at any point.'

'I could—but you seemed to be having such fun.'

'Fun that isn't part of my royal duties...'

The words faded away from her tongue, leaving her mouth dry and tight.

'I was having…you saw?'

Karim didn't condescend to give her an answer, but his total stillness told her all she needed to know.

'You followed me!'

He didn't even blink.

'I came here to fetch you back to Rhastaan. It is my duty to make sure that you arrive there safely and in time for the wedding ceremony.'

Something in the word 'safely' caught on a raw edge of Clemmie's nerves, making her frown in uncertainty. But there was something else that had slid into her mind, something that now seemed to explode in a shock reaction.

'You followed me—you saw where I was—you saw I was…h-having fun.' So had he seen Harry too? Had he looked through the window and seen the obvious affection she had for the little boy and he for her? Could he now tell someone…?

'But you didn't fetch me from there. You watched and then you came back here and waited for me to come home. Why?'

'I have been asking myself that too.'

'And how have you answered it?'

Another of those expressive shoulder shrugs but this time it was not just dismissive. Instead she would have said that it had a touch of uncertainty about it except that uncertainty was not something she could possibly associate with Karim in any way.

'I wanted to see what would happen.'

'But if I hadn't come back—if I'd stayed or moved on somewhere else… No, don't answer that!'

She caught the gleam of something disturbing and dangerous in that rough-hewn face. Something that the flickering candlelight made even more worrying as it cast shadows across his stunning features. She knew what would have happened if she'd tried anything else. He would have come after her like the hunting cat she'd imagined him to be earlier, and when he'd caught up with her...

Something cold and nasty slid down her spine at just the thought of what would have happened then. But, in the same moment, her pulse also jumped at the image of him coming after her, hunting her down, making her his.

Oh—that was stupid! Quite the most impossible image! If this man hunted her down, it was only to collect her and take her back to another man—to her prospective bridegroom. And he was only doing that because of this strongly felt sense of *duty* that he kept harping on about. Did she need any further evidence that he had never considered her as a person in all this, but only as the 'target', the errant princess he must return to her arranged marriage, no consideration as to whether she was willing or not coming into it?

'Tell me something...why is it that you are here—? Yes, I know you've told me that you've come to escort me back to Nabil. But why *you*? Surely there must be other security men—other people you could have sent to fetch me.'

Other security men who wouldn't have disturbed her as much as this man did. Who wouldn't have sparked off these wild, sensual fantasies that had been plaguing her ever since Karim had walked into her life.

'Why you?'

She'd touched on some raw nerve there; the change in his face, in his stance, gave it all away. He swung to-

wards the windows, pulling the curtains closed on the
night with a rough, jerky movement. With the reflected
light of the snow shut out, the small room seemed even
darker and more confined, claustrophobically so, and
Karim's lean muscular body filled the space with a sense
of power that it seemed impossible the tiny cottage could
contain. Clemmie didn't know if the tiny hairs at the back
of her neck had lifted in apprehension or excitement. She
only knew that it suddenly seemed as if the heat from the
fire couldn't reach her and she was shivering in shock
and reaction.

'My father had promised Nabil's family that he would
make sure you reached Rhastaan safely. He owed them
that, after Nabil's father had saved his life once in a he-
licopter accident. It was a matter of honour.'

And that honour meant more than any consideration
of the person he was dealing with. The need to get her
back to Rhastaan overriding anything else.

'But he has been taken ill—heart problems—that
meant he had to hand the task over to someone else.'

And that was all she was. 'The task' who would be
handed over like a parcel that needed delivery. If he
had stabbed a knife between her ribs he couldn't have
wounded her more.

'And only you could keep that honour? You don't have
the loyalty of your own security team?'

If she'd picked up her glass of water and flung it in his
face, he couldn't have reacted more sharply. It was as if
she was watching a metal door slamming closed behind
his eyes, shutting her off from everything in his thoughts,
blanking out his expression completely.

'You don't!'

The realisation was sharp, shocking like a stab of light

into her mind and closing off her throat, taking her breath with it.

'You can't trust your own men.'

Her voice came and went like a radio with faulty tuning and the strength seemed to be draining from her legs, seeping away from her, leaving her trembling with shock.

'My father's men.' Karim's tone was flat, totally deadpan, his face mirroring his expressionless response. 'Or, rather, one—as far as we know for now. We found that he was working for Ankhara.'

Ankhara. The man whose very name was a threat to her own security, who was determined to prevent the marriage to Nabil from going ahead. Who wouldn't let a mere woman stand in the way of his ruthless ambition.

Surely the room couldn't have got so very much colder in the space of several uneven heartbeats? The fire in the hearth was burning brighter than ever but the heat didn't seem to be reaching out to her. Instead she was chilled right through to the bone.

'And he was the one who was supposed to come and fetch me?'

A brusque, curt nod was his only answer, not a word being spoken.

'So you came instead of him.'

To make sure that the job was done properly. Because of that sense of honour he had referred to. The cold that was creeping through her body was there because of her own fault. Somewhere along the line, weakly, foolishly, she had allowed herself to think, to dream, however briefly, that there was the possibility that Karim had come to protect her specially. That he had cared just a little bit because—because it was her? What sort of foolishness had she let creep into her thoughts, making her feel that she *mattered*? At least to him. But the truth was that she mattered to no one.

It was a matter of honour.

Karim's honour, and that of his father, his country. The country where he now was Crown Prince after the loss of his brother. He took that role very seriously, it seemed.

CHAPTER SIX

THE SMALL ROOM seemed to shrink even more, the darkness closing in around her as she faced up to the truth of what was happening. She was just a pawn in so many political games. She wasn't a person, just a piece on a political chessboard. She shivered convulsively, unable to hold back the instinctive response to her thoughts.

'Are you cold?' Those sharp black eyes had caught her reaction, and he was moving forward hastily. 'Shall I put some more coal on the fire—build it up?'

'No.' Her shake of the head was determined, almost wild, sending her hair flying around her face. 'No, thanks.'

All she wanted was to go away and hide somewhere, go into the darkness with her thoughts. Close her eyes and try to hold on to that last image of Harry as he waved from the window when she had driven off. The last time she would ever see the baby brother she was doing this for. Surely Karim, who said that he had lost a brother too—and in a far more permanent way—would understand.

But then she looked up into those opaque eyes, all emotion wiped away—if there had ever been any there in the first place—and she knew that she was dreaming even more if she allowed herself to think that he even saw her as a person. She was that point of honour that had to be dealt with. He would do his duty, deliver her to wherever she needed to be—where he needed her to be—and then he would go on his way and forget her, never even looking back for a second.

'I'm tired,' she managed, avoiding the real issue that tormented her. 'I want to go to bed—to sleep.'

He didn't even try to hide the way he looked at his watch, checking the time, and just that single sidelong glance told its own story, reminding her of the frequent occasions on which he had done just that already tonight. Checking his phone, his computer, frustrated by the delay that kept them trapped here together. Impatient and anxious to be on his way. To get this matter of duty over and done with, the responsibility that his father had passed on to him, handed over to the people who really wanted her.

And then he could go home, satisfied that he had done his duty. Honour would be served.

'Yes, I know it's early,' she snapped, flinging her own scathing glance at the grandfather clock in the corner, its large white face only barely revealed in the flickering light of the flames. 'But I'm tired. I had a late night last night. I was talking with my friends,' she added with even more of an edge as she saw his dark head come up, black eyes narrowing sharply as he stared at her down the long, straight beak of his nose, nostrils actually flaring as if he had caught some distasteful smell just beneath them.

Harry had been restless, overexcited by the party and then unhappy at the thought that she was going away, that his beloved Clemmie would be leaving in the morning and was unlikely to be coming back. In order to let Mary have a much needed night's sleep, and to indulge herself with one last long night together before those dreadful final farewells, she had sat with the little boy, reading him story after story, and then finally rocking him to sleep in her arms. She had been so afraid of disturbing him that she had sat there for over an hour until she had felt that she could ease herself away and leave him sleeping. As a result she had barely had more than a couple of hours' rest herself.

'We could do something...'

Karim cursed himself for letting the truth about the situation with Ankhara slip. It had had exactly the result he had dreaded, set her off in a panic so that now she was restless and unsettled as a nervous cat. He doubted very much that she would be likely to sleep as she had declared, even though the shadows under her eyes did seem to speak of her need to rest. They had darkened since he had seen her first, making him wonder just what had happened in the days since he had arrived at the cottage. What had happened last night? He had waited, watched, until all the lights in the house had gone out, but all he had seen before that was some kid's party, and, later, a group of mothers arriving to take their little ones home.

'And what, exactly, would you propose?' Her head was flung back, huge eyes widening even more as she faced him. 'Play some music, perhaps. Or watch a film on DVD—oh, no, I forgot—we don't have any electricity, do we. So that's a no then.'

'We could talk.'

Talk! What the hell was he thinking about even suggesting it? Talking meant her moving her lips, drawing attention to the wideness of her mouth, the soft fullness of those rose-tinted lips. Every time she spoke, or when she had opened her mouth to eat or drink, all he had been able to think of had been the way those lips would feel under his, how they would part to the pressure of his tongue. How her mouth would taste deep inside, warm and moist in an intimate caress.

It was all he could do now not to stare fixedly at that mouth, or reach out a hand to trace a finger along the bow shape of her lips.

'Talk? No, thanks. I've had enough lectures on duty and honour from you and everyone else to last me a lifetime.'

He'd missed a beat, watching her lips and tongue frame those words, wanting...

'Something else then.' He sounded as if he'd swallowed broken glass, his throat husky and raw, so that she frowned at him when she heard it.

'Something else?' She rolled her eyes in exasperation. 'Precisely what? Oh—perhaps you'd like to try a board game—I know Nan has some somewhere. A little old-fashioned looking but they don't really change, do they? Can I challenge you to a game of Ludo or perhaps you'd prefer Snakes and Ladders?'

She couldn't make it plainer that she was being sarcastic, but he couldn't resist taking her up on it, teasing her deliberately.

'Why not? If that's what's available. And I've never played either of those—I have to admit to being intrigued to find out just what sort of game goes by the name of—Ludo? And what the devil is Serpents and Ladders?'

'Snakes. It's a board game—they both are. And you're not going to convince me that you actually want...'

'Oh, but I do.'

The look she turned on him as she tested the truth of his assertion was impatience, indignation and total disbelief all in one. The trouble was that it was pure provocation at the same time, the wicked gleam in her eyes, the faint curl at the corner of her mouth. He hoped to hell that these ridiculously named games would have something to hold his attention, distract him from looking at her, keeping his eyes on the board or something so that he wasn't so tempted.

Her little hiss of irritation was so appealing that it was worth having suggested this just to hear it, and to see the spark in her eyes as she told him without words that he was going to regret this. The pert challenge of her rear pushing against the denim of her jeans as she bent over a drawer in the sideboard to pull out the box of games was much more difficult to resist and his palms itched to smooth across the taut buttocks, curving over the swell of her hips.

Hell—no! That was the way to destruction and devastation. Why did the one woman to make him this hot and hard in so long have to be the woman who was barred from him? The woman who would destroy his honour and that of his family—his country—if he tangled with her. It would be one hell of a lot easier if she wasn't giving off signals that a blind man could read at a hundred paces. She was as drawn to him as he was to her, but they could not, they *must* not act on it.

Needing to hide the brutally physical effect she was having on him, he sat down hard on the settee she had just vacated and forced his attention on to the boxes she had lifted from the drawer. It wasn't easy. The swing of her hair as she placed the boxes on the table brushed against his face in a way that was a torment to his heightened senses, and her position as she bent to open the top gave a savagely tempting glimpse of the shadowed valley of her cleavage and the creamy curves of her breasts. Only by digging his teeth hard into his lower lip, almost drawing blood, did he manage to hold back his groan of primitive response.

'So tell me the rules…because there are rules, I presume?'

Weren't there always rules? Rules that ran your life on regimented lines. Rules that would cause chaos if broken. The scar on his chest stung as if in response to his thoughts and he rubbed at it abstractedly. If he had needed any reminder of what happened when the rules got twisted and shattered, it was right there, underneath his shirt, etched into his skin. His life had been built on loyalty. Loyalty to his father, to his older brother the Crown Prince, to his country. Those had been the rules— until he'd bent them so that his brother could ease up on the protocol he fretted at. As a result, those rules had been blown so wide apart that new ones had to be put in their place.

And Razi was dead, his reputation buried with him.

But at least these rules were simple. It was, after all, just a child's game, with die and counters, cartoon images of brightly coloured snakes, ladders of various lengths. It did help to distract him—barely. The truth was that he could play the game with just one quarter of his concentration, the rest he tried to fix on other matters—keeping the fire alight, removing the guttering stubs of candles and replacing them with new ones, checking his phone, his computer, to see if the connection had been restored. It never had, only adding an extra mental burn to the rage of his physical frustration.

At the same time, there was a strangely intense relaxation in what he was doing. If someone had told him at the start of this mission that he would end up sitting opposite the gorgeous, sexy, beddable woman he had been sent to collect—playing a child's game and actually *enjoying it*, Karim told himself half an hour or so later, he would never have believed them. And if they had told him that the woman he was sitting opposite was the woman who made his body harden and hunger in a way no woman in the rest of the world had ever done—and he hadn't been able to do a thing about it— he would have declared that they were crazy. Totally out of their heads. There was no way he was going to accept any mission that put him into such a position, and to hell with the repercussions.

But no one had told him, no one had warned him. And he was here, now, with irresistible temptation in the female form sitting opposite—so close—too close—and he was having to clamp down hard on every carnal impulse that made him a man.

But at least she had calmed down. She seemed to have pushed away the realisation that there was a possible threat to her, a danger from the plotters and manipulators who didn't want her marriage to go ahead. She had lost that look of the startled rabbit caught in the headlights of an oncoming car, and she was focusing on the game. She was also fiercely competitive, biting her lip in disappointment when she hit a snake, or crowing in delight when he did the same, especially when it was the longest snake on the board.

'Down!' She laughed, the sound tangling round his insides and pulling hard. 'Go on—right down to thirteen again! I'm going to win this game.'

'Not if I can help it!'

Glancing up into Karim's face, lit for a moment then shadowed again as the flames played over his features,

Clemmie saw the way his mouth had softened slightly, his eyes less like deep black ice. He thought he'd settled her down, she knew. He believed he had distracted her from the thought that out there, in the wildness of the storm, someone was hunting them—hunting her. And he had almost succeeded.

He'd be doing a better job of it if he wasn't so intent on looking at his phone, tapping the screen of his tablet, to check on what was happening. The small frequent movement set her teeth on edge, reminding her that not all was as peaceful and warm as the small firelit room.

And yet, in the strangest way, she felt a relaxation such as she had never known before. Not since she had played these games with her grandmother. The simple moves of the game, the heat of the fire, the flickering light of the candles, all created an enclosed space, a sanctuary, where there was just the two of them, and the rest of the world was shut out beyond the thick stone walls of the cottage. The desultory conversation drifted over a range of topics, nothing too deep, nothing too controversial. She had never felt so free in her life. Never believed that she could actually say what she wanted, express herself openly, and not be slapped down verbally as she was at court, or warned with a black frown or worse from her father if she ventured into forbidden territory.

She even felt comfortable with the physical sensations that were racing through her body, stinging at her nerves, as she shared this confined space with the big dark man who had invaded her life. She *wanted* to know the fizz of excitement that made it almost impossible to sit still. She wanted to hear the rough texture of his voice scraping across her skin, allow herself the luxury of leaning forward, apparently to move her counter over the board, but in fact to inhale the scent of his body and let it intoxicate her in the most sensual way.

'Five…'

Karim totted up the number of dots on the bright red die and counted the spaces as he moved his counter along, narrowly missing the same long ladder that had taken her own token almost within reach of the end goal. She was so intent on watching his long-fingered hand, the tanned skin, the clean, cared-for nails…imagining what that strength, that control would feel like on her own skin, how it would be if it lost control, that her breath quickened in her lungs, her mouth drying fast.

'My turn…'

As she reached for the die and the shaker, her hand touched his, the burn of electricity sizzling over every nerve, making her gasp in uncontrolled shock.

'What?'

His dark head came up sharply, black eyes burning into hers so that she almost flinched away from their force on her skin.

'N—nothing…'

Her voice cracked and broke in the middle as she tried to swallow to ease the tension in her throat.

'My turn,' she managed again.

'OK—no!'

It was worse this time because he reached out to still her hand, long fingers closing over hers, warm and hard and… She tensed herself to pull away, then found she couldn't make herself do it.

'Not your turn—not yet. I have to…'

His attention was back on the board, allowing her a moment to snatch in a much needed breath. Was it confusion or the rush of loss as he released her hand that clouded her thoughts? Karim was counting again.

'Thought so.'

Blankly, she watched as he took his counter back to his original square on the board and one elegant finger stabbed at the following numbers. Then he moved his token, not to the long ladder but to one of the most fearsome-looking snakes and slid down it, right to the tip of its tail, six rows below.

It took a couple of unsteady heartbeats for her to realise what she had just seen and to count back again, checking it out.

'That's five,' she managed at last.

'And I originally made a mistake and counted six. It's fine now.'

'You didn't have to.' Was the snow falling even more heavily outside, whipped up by the wind, or was that the race of her heart pulsing in her ears? 'I hadn't noticed.'

Of course she hadn't noticed. She'd been so busy watching him, watching his hands, the down-dropped lids as he focused on the board. The jet-black arc of his long lashes resting above those knife-sharp cheekbones, shadowing the olive skin. She'd been watching the movement of his lips as he counted the squares, imagining how it would feel, how it would taste to have those lips on hers. *Wanting* his mouth on hers.

'I didn't see…'

Her tongue stumbled over the words, tangling up on itself so that she wasn't sure that what she said was even comprehensible.

'But I did—'

His eyes lifted again, seeming to spear her on his intent gaze. Hot colour flashed over her skin, making it burn so fiercely that she was grateful for the flickering shadows that hid the changing colour of her complexion.

'And if I had not corrected it, it would have been cheating.'

He made it sound like the worst sin possible.

'And you are such a man of honour.'

The look he turned on her made ice drops skitter down her spine. It was both challenge and agreement. *Don't ever doubt it*, he might have said, and she *didn't* doubt it. How could she possibly? But there was a darkness and a tension behind the words that tightened her throat in a sense of apprehension at the thought of something coming closer, growing more dangerous, like a premonition that would affect her life in an ominously threatening way.

Feeling cold through to the bone in a way that no warmth from the fire could banish, she forced her eyes away from his, focusing intently on the board in front of her. Up another ladder, down a snake…straight up to the last few numbers and then…

'I won!'

The triumph was a soaring rush of adrenalin, a dangerous mix with the fast beat of her heart, the hungry need she had never known before. And yet, underneath it all, that worrying chill still lingered disturbingly.

'You won…' Karim conceded and then he took all that triumph and excitement away, leaving only the chill, by yet another glance at his watch, his phone. 'Another game?'

'No, thanks. I'm tired.'

It was true. With the rushing away of all that heated response, pushed from her soul by bitter disappointment at the realisation that her imaginings were just that—

fantasy—she felt drained and lost, bone-weary. She nerved herself for the sarcastic comment—something on the lines of running away—or hiding.

It didn't come. Instead, with another of those infuriating glances at his watch, Karim simply nodded, picking up the counters, the die, and tossing them back into the box.

It was like riding some emotional roller coaster, one moment allowing herself to go up, up into the heady air of believing he was interested—that he might know something of the way she was feeling, and experience it too. Only to be knocked right back down again in the space of a heartbeat as one more casual glance at his watch told its own story.

The relaxed, enjoyable evening—the evening she *had thought* was relaxed and enjoyable but in fact had probably just been him tolerating her, going along with things to pass the time and distract her, was over. She was dismissed, his thoughts turning to something else entirely. He didn't have to say that all he wanted was to get out of here and deliver her to her husband-to-be. It was written into every action he took, hidden under the careful mask of politeness.

Now she really was tired. She felt like a balloon when all the air had escaped from a small leak, limp and flat, but the thought of heading up into the icebox that was her bedroom held no appeal at all. Karim was moving, getting to his feet, picking up cushions from the settee, dropping them on to the floor.

'What are you doing?'

'Your bed.' A wave of his hand indicated the sofa. 'Mine.' This time he gestured towards the cushions at his feet. 'You don't want to freeze upstairs.'

'N—no...' It was disconcerting, almost as if he had read her thoughts.

'A bit of a tight fit, but it will have to do. I'll get some blankets.'

She had been tired, but would she be able to sleep now? Clemmie asked herself when, a few minutes later, she was ensconced on the settee and firmly wrapped in the blankets Karim had brought down from the bedroom. She was cosy enough—physically at least—but a sneaking chill was winding its way around her thoughts.

Was Karim really acting out of consideration for her or was he merely settling there on the floor to keep a watch over her, make sure she didn't attempt another escape during the night? She'd freeze to death if she did; the knee-length pink tee shirt style nightdress she had pulled on was modest enough but no protection against the bitter night, but clearly he didn't trust her. Turning restlessly on the lumpy sofa, she fought to get comfortable. It was impossible to get her thoughts straight on Karim. One moment he seemed to care just a bit. The next she was sure he was only doing that duty he believed was so important. Her eyes went to where Karim still sat in the one chair, a black, bulky figure in the darkness. Now that the candles had been extinguished for safety, the only light came from the glow of the fire, banked down ready to last through the night. His arms rested along his thighs, shoulders hunched forward as he stared into the grate. Was she destined only ever to have ambiguous feelings about him?

That thought made her stomach clench at the realisation that her time with him was ebbing away fast. Once the dawn came he would find some way of getting the car moved, getting them on their way. And if the future had seemed grim enough before, the thought of the loveless political marriage she had to make hovering like a black cloud on the horizon, now the prospect of getting there and watching Karim walk away out of her life seemed impossible, unbearable. How had he come to mean so much to her in such a short space of time? And how could she let him go when they reached Rhastaan?

Let him go! Burying her face in the blanket, she forced back the bite of acid in her mouth. She wouldn't *let* him go. *She* would have no part of it. He would just turn and walk away from her. Job done. Duty fulfilled. Not a single look back.

Somehow she fell asleep but in her dreams there were dark shapes and shadows haunting her mind, chasing after her. She was running, calling out for Karim, but he was ahead of her. Always ahead of her, walking away, and no matter how fast she tried to run, he was always so far ahead of her even though he was just walking. But her father and Ankhara were behind her, catching her up, coming closer with every step they took.

'No…' She wished she could shake them off but they were coming closer. 'No—*no*!'

'Clementina…'

Someone had caught up with her, caught her. They were holding her arm, shaking her…

'Clementina.'

She knew that voice—recognised it… A rush of memory jolted her awake, bringing her upright in shock, eyes wide, staring into the dark face that had haunted all her dreams but only because it had always been turned away from her. Now he was here, so close, perched on the edge of the settee, his hands closed about her arms, the heat of his palms burning into her skin. He had discarded his sweater and the trousers he had been wearing, his only covering a white tee shirt and dark boxers. She could barely see his features in the shadows but the dark pools of his eyes drew her in.

He was too close. She was drowning. She could hardly breathe, the little air she could snatch in tangling in her throat as she stared up at him. And that air was touched with the scent of his skin, still warm from the blankets he'd been sleeping in.

'What happened?'

'I—was scared. Ankhara…'

Hell, he'd really messed up, Karim reproached himself, telling her about Ankhara. Nightmares were bad enough; the thrashing of her body and the way she'd moaned in her sleep had brought him awake fast. She'd been dreaming about the man who'd sent men after them. Who would try to put a stop to this marriage if he possibly could.

'It's all right.'

Did she know what it did to him to see the way her eyes had widened, deep as lakes in the whiteness of her face? How could he ever have thought her the wild, careless party girl she'd been described to him as? The woman who had carelessly tossed her duty to her family, to her country, aside when she had set out to seek her own pleasure, heedless of anyone else? There was more to it than that. Another reason why she had come here. He didn't know what it was but he was sure there was something underneath her apparent recklessness. Perhaps it was something to do with this Harry—whoever he was. A friend? A lover?

'Clementina, it's all right—you're safe.'

And she would be safe if he had anything to do with

it, he vowed inwardly. He would make sure she reached Rhastaan safely if it was the last thing he did. He didn't allow himself to acknowledge that that vow was made for Clementina herself, not just for the debt he owed to Nabil's family.

'C-Clemmie…' Her voice was low and husky, that trace of breathlessness still lingering in a way that tugged at his nerves.

'What?'

'Clemmie,' she said again, more strongly this time. 'My—friends—call me Clemmie.'

'Is that what we are? Friends?'

The battle he was having with the sexual hunger that had flared as soon as he had taken her in his arms to waken her made his question rough and raw, catching on her mood, changing it in a second. She frowned, bit down on the softness of her lower lip as she considered, then shrugged in a way he couldn't interpret. Not with his head full of forbidden thoughts of how he wanted to reach out and ease her lips apart, stop her from injuring the soft flesh. He wanted to soothe the injury she was inflicting on herself with the sweep of his tongue. She was so close, the scent of her body so warm that he could almost taste her on each breath he drew in, and the cotton boxers provided little or no concealment of the aching hardness that those thoughts, the enticement of her body had built between his legs.

'If that's how you want it,' she muttered. 'After all, what else could we be?'

'What else indeed,' he agreed, nodding slowly. Then, seeing her shiver in the night air, he frowned sharply. 'You should get back under the blankets—go to sleep.'

Her eyes met his, shadowed and defiant.

'I don't want to sleep. I'm afraid that if I close my eyes it will all come back again.'

'But you need to rest…' And he needed to get the hell away from her before he gave in to the carnal thoughts that were frying his brain.

'Couldn't you hold me?'

It was the last thing he had expected, the last thing he needed, and it knocked him off balance for a moment, almost reeling back where he sat.

'Clemmie…' His voice was thick, rough, and it was only when he heard himself say it that he realised he had conceded and used the name she wanted him to call her.

Her pink tongue slicked over her lips, leaving behind a gleam of moisture that had a kick of cruel temptation out of all proportion to its size. Hunger clawed at him, forcing him to clamp his mouth shut on a groan of response.

'Please hold me. Just till I get back to sleep.'

She moved the blanket aside, opening a space under it for him to join her, and the movement revealed the slender pale length of her legs, the sight draining all the moisture from his mouth in a second. He tried to speak, to tell her how crazy this would be—how *wrong*—but his voice failed him and she was already talking again, taking his silence for some sort of concession of agreement.

'I don't think I could possibly sleep if you don't. And you must be cold out there in what you're wearing.'

He was cold. In spite of the fire, there was no real warmth in the air and he was thinking longingly of being under the blankets and huddling into them.

But the truth was that he was also thinking more longingly of being under the blankets *with her* and holding her close. In spite of the cold, his body burned at the thought.

'*Please*,' she said again in a voice that took all his strength from him.

He was lost.

CHAPTER SEVEN

'IF YOU PROMISE to go to sleep…'

'I promise.'

Surely this was hell, Karim told himself as she scooted over and he eased himself into the small space that she had left for him. Hell was not eternal fire or demons torturing you. Hell was a cosy nest in a too-small bed with a woman he ached to possess but was forbidden to touch. He could only pray that she would go to sleep fast.

'How am I supposed to sleep with you sitting there like you have a broom handle for a spine?' Clemmie protested, the warmth of her breath shivering over his skin.

'There's not much room…'

'Then curl up closer…'

She suited actions to the words, her movement building the heat in their little cocoon to boiling point. Damn it, was she really that naïve or—his heart skipped a beat with a heavy thud—was she doing this deliberately?

'Sleep!' he growled roughly, his lips brushing the silky hair on the top of her head, fine strands catching on his skin, on the roughness of his day-old stubble as they did so.

Sleep!

Clemmie barely caught back the word of protest as she

let her face rest against his chest. How was she expected to sleep like this? Her whole body was wildly awake, her heart pounding, her breathing suddenly raw and heavy in her lungs. The strength of the arms holding her were at once a source of comfort and dangerous excitement and the hard bones of his ribcage seemed to be made specially to support her head. The heat of his skin had turned the comfort she had been looking for into an inferno of need that pulsed between her legs in a way she had never known before.

This then was *desire*. This was what it felt like to want a man—this particular man—in the way that a woman was meant to feel.

She wanted—*needed*—to feel more of him. One hand stroking across the white cotton of his tee shirt, she could feel the thud of his heart under her fingertips, the smoothness of skin, the...

The movement stilled, her head lifting slightly, at the unexpected thickening and roughness where everywhere else there had been smooth skin.

'What's this?'

'Clemmie—'

She caught the note of warning but ignored it. Her fingers brushed against the swollen hardness of his lower body as she pushed at the hem of his tee shirt at his waist. It almost made her pause, the realisation of what it meant sending shockwaves of reaction through every inch of her. But the new and very different tension in the powerful body beside her told her that she was touching on something that mattered, something that came close to the innermost part of this man, and she was not to be put off.

'What's wrong?'

She pushed the white cotton aside, bunching it up around his shoulders and then caught her breath in shock at what she had exposed.

'Damn it, Clemmie…'

With a muttered curse, Karim twisted sharply, catching hold of her wrists and imprisoning them in the strength of his hands. But not before she had registered what was there. Even in the dim light from the fire, the disfiguring ridges and lines were plain to see. The scars that marked one side of his chest, marring the sleek beauty of the bronzed skin, untouched by the haze of crisp black hair that covered so much of his torso.

'But what happened? When?'

He was only relatively newly healed. The scars were still pink and new, not yet easing into the silvery lines that followed the softening effects of time.

'How?'

He wasn't going to answer; she could see it in the set of his face, the way that his beautiful mouth was clamped tight shut, the red burn of the fire throwing shadows on and off the hard planes of his cheeks.

She'd seen that sort of tension once before. When he had spoken of his brother and the fact that he had died. The scars were connected with that incident; she had no doubt of that. Karim didn't need to say a word; the emotional truth was etched on to his face, no matter how much he might want to dodge away from her seeking eyes.

He didn't try, though. Instead he met her questioning gaze head-on, the light of challenge flaring in the darkness of his eyes. His grip on her wrists had softened now, letting her ease herself away, and Clemmie let her fingertips drift over the damaged skin, her breath catching as she saw the change in his face, the way his eyelids dropped briefly to shut himself off from her.

'What happened to your brother? I mean—I know he died in a car crash, but—you were there, weren't you?'

'I was in the car behind.'

He sounded as if the words had been dragged out of him. If it hadn't been for the darkness, the silence of the night, she wouldn't have caught the words, they were so low, so soft.

'He wanted to see a woman—not the woman he was betrothed to marry. So he'd dismissed the security detail, but I couldn't let him go out without any protection. I followed him.'

A long pause, another obvious effort to make himself go on.

'I made the mistake of letting him see me in the mirror so he drove too fast to get away from me. He took a bend carelessly… By the time I reached them his car was on fire.'

'And you tried to get him out.'

It wasn't a question; it was a statement. She knew without any sort of doubt that that was how he had been injured, scarred.

'I…'

Whatever he had been about to say was choked off as she bent her head to press her lips to his wounded skin, acknowledging silently the way he must have tried—the horror of having failed as the fire had driven him back. Softly she kissed her way over the long scar, acknowledging the courage it must have taken to earn it.

'Clementina…'

Her name hissed in between his teeth but she barely heard it. She was lost, drugged on the taste of him, the scent of his skin. Her tongue slid over the ridges of the scar, tasting the slightly salty tang of his skin, and she heard the beat of his heart quicken and deepen, sounding like thunder in her ears. Her own heart was racing, primitive feelings, sensations she had never known before stirring deep inside her, pulsing between her legs. She wanted to crawl on top of Karim, hold him, lose herself in him.

This was what sexual hunger was all about; why it was spoken of in those tones that had made her feel it could never be as powerful or as intense as it was implied. But the way she was feeling now told her that she had underestimated its force, its potential for wild abandonment. The room had faded into blackness, the faint crackle of the fire barely audible in her ears. There was only her and this man…this man who made her feel what it was really like to be a woman.

'Clemmie…'

It was raw and rough, a sound of protest or surrender and she couldn't tell which. But then his hands tangled in her hair, yanking her face up to his.

The mood in the room changed totally in the space of an uneven heartbeat. This wasn't warm or gentle or even considerate. It was dark and harsh and dangerous. Everything about Karim was hard. His facial features seemed to have been carved from stone. His mouth was clamped into a tight forceful line, his chest and arms were like rocks against her cheeks. And the erection that she was crushed up against was like burning steel, threatening to brand her as his.

'Damn you, woman!' he muttered again and the last word came out harshly against her lips as his head swooped and his mouth took hers, crushing her lips back against her teeth as he plundered the softness between them.

His hands were tighter in her hair now, holding her head, twisting it till it was in the perfect position where he wanted it. The perfect position for his kiss. A kiss that was like nothing she had ever known before.

Their mouths fused and everything Clemmie had thought she had known about male and female inter-action, about sexual interest or excitement was obliter-ated from her mind in one explosive moment. This was nothing like the tentative clumsy, or even the pushy se-cret kisses of the few boys she had met at college. There was nothing boyish about this at all. It was all male, the hunger of a fully grown man, and it roused all that was woman in her. It had such force and power, such heat, that it was like being kissed by a volcano. It was the kiss of a man who knew what he wanted and was determined to take it.

And what he wanted was her.

Clemmie's mind was spinning, whirling, her ability to think spiralling off into the darkness somewhere so that she could no longer keep track of it. Somewhere under the molten lava in her mind, created by Karim's kiss, firing her blood, was a warning thought that she should not let this happen; that she should say no and push him away. Push herself away. But that weak protesting thought was drowned out by the stronger, fiercer need that thundered along every nerve, pounding at her temples, driving away any other sort of awareness.

It was wild and carnal, primitive in the extreme, but it was what she wanted now. It was all that she wanted. Karim was all that she wanted. Karim and his kiss, hot and heavy on her mouth. His touch on her skin, searing a path over her legs, her hips, her waist, heading inexorably upwards, towards her aching breasts, the hardened nipples hungry for his caress.

His possession...

Something blew a fuse in Clemmie's thoughts, forcing her to realise that the modest tee shirt nightie was no longer anything like so modest. It was no barrier at all to those urgently seeking fingers. Her nightdress was rucked up well past her waist, her naked legs were tangled with his, smooth skin against the muscular power of long, hair-covered masculine limbs. The feel of his hot skin under her hands was like bathing in liquid fire. She wanted to touch all of him, kiss all of him, feel all of him, all at one time.

'Karim...'

She mouthed his name against his skin, taking in the taste of him as she muttered the word. The hair on his chest pricked at her tongue, soft electrical impulses that made her shiver in response. She needed to writhe nearer, pressing herself against the length of his body.

Karim muttered something in a language she didn't understand, his teeth grazing her neck softly, and with a sudden movement he took possession of the breasts he had exposed to his caresses, making Clemmie gasp aloud and rear up slightly, flinging back her head in a rush of response. But a moment later she regretted the slight break of contact, needing more, so that she dropped her face down to his again, her hair forming a soft curtain around them as she took the kiss she wanted—needed.

The heat of his erection pressed against the moist curls between her legs, but her body hungered for more. She yearned to feel the full heat and power of him without even the barrier of his underwear, fine though it was.

With a hungry murmur deep in her throat, she slipped her hands between them, finding the elasticated waistband and tugging at it, wanting to draw it down. She felt the tension in his body in a new and disturbing way; one she wanted to ignore because she was afraid of what it meant.

'Clemmie! No!'

Karim bucked underneath her, his reaction as violent as if he had been stung. And what she feared was there in his tone, in the warning she didn't want to hear.

'Hellfire, lady... I— No! *I said no!*'

He twisted away, caught her hands again and held them prisoner at the wrist. She could feel his heart thudding against his ribcage and knew that he was every bit as aroused as she was, every bit as hungry. But he was determined to deny it.

'Karim!' she protested, her voice thick with need. 'Don't do this. I want you—why are you doing this?'

The breath he snatched in was raw and ragged, grating its way into his lungs.

'We can't do this. We must not. You know why.'

She knew he was trying to appeal to her sense of reason but it wasn't going to work. She didn't want it to work. She didn't feel at all reasonable. She *wanted* this. Wanted it with every beat of her heart.

'Do I?'

Deliberately she wriggled against him, smiling under the cover of her hair as she heard his groan, felt the tension in the long body beside her.

'I don't see why. This is almost the last night of my single life—my last night of freedom—surely I can spend it as I want—with who I want.'

'If you were anyone else, then yes.'

His voice scraped over her nerves, waking restraints

and scruples that had never been there before. It was as if someone had lifted away the blankets, doused the fire, and the cold, creeping sense of misery that oozed over her skin was almost overwhelming.

Almost. But underneath the sense of hesitation that chilled the heat of her hunger there was another, more rebellious feeling that flared and burned away her qualms. It throbbed to the beat of the pulse between her legs, impossible to deny.

She had spent her life living according to her father's calculated rules. Settlements that had been decided for her and about her but without any consent or even knowledge on her part. She hadn't even *lived* her life. It had all been dictated for her by her parent's ambition. But here, tonight, she had one chance—her only chance—to live as other women her age had the freedom to live. The freedom to…

No—her thoughts danced away from the dangerous four-letter word she had almost allowed into her mind. There was no love in this.

She couldn't fall in love in less than forty-eight hours with a man who had been a stranger until she had opened the door to him—was it really only yesterday? It wasn't love; it was lust—but lust was a new and exciting feeling. One she had never experienced before. One she was sure she was never likely to feel when she was forced into a diplomatic marriage with a man she didn't know. No, not a man—a boy—nearly five years younger than her.

She would never experience the joy and excitement of falling in love. But she could experience *this*. It might be all she would ever have to sustain her in the arid, desolate years that lay ahead.

'But we are who we are and this can never be. It is forbidden. You are forbidden.'

'Not tonight.'

Increasing anxiety, the nagging ache of withdrawal as the stinging excitement ebbed painfully, leaving every inch of her burning and hungry, made her voice desperate.

'Tonight we are just two people, alone in the dark. This cottage is miles from anywhere, and the snow has isolated us even more. There's no one to see us, no one to know.'

'We would know.' His voice sounded as if it was fraying at the edges. 'I would know.'

'But we need never…'

Something about his terrible stillness, the way his head was turned away from her, his eyes refusing to meet hers, staring into the fire instead, sent a shaft of ice slicing through her. It froze her into an immobility to match his, her heart quailing deep inside.

'Is it—'

She couldn't manage to say it, didn't want to say it. But it had to be faced. In her naiveté, had she made the most terrible mistake, imagining something that wasn't there? Had she put her own longings on to the moment, creating a scenario she wanted, but one that had never been there at all?

'Don't you want me?'

Karim's answer was a deep, soul-felt groan.

'Not want you?' He was almost laughing when he said it. But it was a laugh that broke in the middle.

'Not want you? Dear God, lady, but does this…' he turned so that the heat and hardness of his erection was pressed against her naked stomach '…feel like I don't want you?'

It felt like the exact opposite so that her heart leapt a little then sank back down again as she saw the hard set lines of his face.

'I want you so much that it's tearing me apart.'

'Then why? Why not? Karim—you want me—I want you. So why can't we…?'

'No!'

It was a wild explosion of sound, underlined by the violent movement of his long frame, pulling away from her and jack-knifing off the settee in a savage rush.

'No. Damn you to hell, woman, you are not going to tempt me this way. This ends now. Once and for all. It's over. Done. It's never going to happen.'

'But…'

In spite of herself, she rose up on to her knees on the cushions, letting the blanket slip away from her to pool around her legs as she held a hand out to him, trying to reach him. She saw those dark eyes sear over her exposed naked body and it felt as if he had actually flayed the skin from her flesh, leaving her raw and bleeding.

'Don't touch me!' he commanded. 'Don't ever touch me again! I want nothing to do with you—nothing but the job I was sent here to do. I will deliver you to Nabil—to your promised husband.' Could he have injected the words with any more venom? 'And then I will never see you again.'

And he would only be happy when that had happened. He didn't have to say the words. They were there in the darkly savage way he spoke, the burn of violent rejection in his eyes.

Already he was turning away from her, grabbing at the jeans and sweater discarded on a nearby chair, pushing himself into them with rough, angry movements. But when he stamped his feet into his boots and headed for the door, Clemmie couldn't just keep silent and watch him go.

'Where are you going?'

'Outside. In case you haven't noticed—it's raining.'

A brusque jerk of his head indicated the windows, where Clemmie now noticed that water rather than snow was lashing against the glass. A slow dawn was starting too, bringing a faint tinge of light to the sky.

'I will get your car moving—or find a connection for the phone.'

He would do it if it killed him. The declaration was stamped into every line of his face, turning every muscle to stone.

'And while I'm out you should get dressed and be ready to leave. I want to be out of here as soon as it's physically possible.'

Out of here and away from her. Or at least on his way to delivering her to Nabil to pay off a debt of honour. He made her sound like a parcel for which someone had paid express delivery. He was not the passionate lover she had dreamed of, nothing but a cold, hard man intent on using her for his own ends, just as her father had done.

Clemmie shivered in the rush of icy air that had flooded into the small room as Karim yanked open the door and she grabbed at the blankets, pulling them up around her, even over her head, huddling into them for protection.

But it wasn't the cold that he had let into the cottage that made her shudder. Instead the feeling came from deep inside, a terrible sensation of rejection and embarrassment at the way she had behaved. Tossed violently on an unknown sea of physical feelings, she had lost all thought of sanity and self-preservation and had thrown herself at him like some wild creature, driven only by her baser instincts.

The blankets were doing no good. She pulled them closer round her, but they felt rough and uncomfortable against her sensitised skin. Every nerve, every sense that Karim had awoken now stung with an arousal that refused to die down. Even the cotton of her nightdress was uncomfortable against her still peaking nipples and so much of her body was an ache of frustrated hunger that it felt like a bruise over every inch of her. She longed to call Karim back, to beg him to reawaken the excitement that had driven all thought from her mind, left her at the mercy of primal needs that were too strong to be contained.

It was no wonder that she had never needed to fight to resist the sort of temptation that she might have been assailed by. She had never known it. Never experienced anything like real temptation before. But one touch, one kiss from this man and all her defences had been blown apart, leaving her gasping and vulnerable, unable to even form the word *No* in her mind, let alone speak it.

But she hadn't needed to say no. Karim had said it for her. Whatever she had felt for him, he had felt nothing of the same. He might have wanted her physically; she was not so naïve as to be unaware of just what the powerful response of his body meant. But he hadn't wanted *her*.

She had thought—had hoped—that she had found a way to ensure that her first time with a man was, if not out of love and truly something special, then at least with someone who made *her* feel special. Someone who excited her like no man had ever done in her life before. And Karim had made her feel that way. His touch had

sent delight through every inch of her body, at least until
he had pushed her from him, rejecting her so violently
that she still felt the bruises on her soul. And instead of a
wonderful, exciting initiation into womanhood, she just
felt grubby and limp, like a discarded rag.

Slowly, awkwardly, Clemmie got to her feet. Her ankle
still ached, though she realised she had forgotten all about
it when she was in Karim's arms. Her legs didn't quite
feel as if they belonged to her and she swayed where she
stood as she tried to gather her strength. She just wanted
to go and hide, but she knew that Karim was not going
to allow that to happen.

If she needed any reminder then the sound from outside brought her head up sharply, knowing she was already on borrowed time. The hiccup and cough of her old
car's engine finally breaking into life, the rattling roar
that told its own tale. Karim had somehow got it started
and very soon he would have moved it out of the way,
freeing his own vehicle to take to the road and drive them
both away from here.

He would expect her to be ready and waiting to go
with him when he came back into the house.

Just for a minute Clemmie considered rebelling. She
would just sit here and...but as the hooded blanket slid
from her head to her shoulders, reminding her that underneath the brown wool she was just about naked, the
tee shirt nightdress still rucked up above her waist, all
the fight went out of her in a rush. She didn't want Karim
coming back and finding her still as he had left her, discarded and unwanted, in a miserable bundle on the sofa.
She would be dressed and on her feet, ready to face him.

Ready to go.

Slowly she looked round at the small shabby room in

the cottage that had been her home for the past months. The place that been her haven, her sanctuary from the negotiations that had taken her life away, the promises that her father had made on her behalf. But it was no longer her sanctuary. In a couple of days it had changed completely and all because of Karim.

Karim had invaded her space, he had taken away her privacy, her security—her self-respect—and nothing would ever be the same again.

So she might as well go now and face the future that lay ahead of her. Her brief, foolish dreams of finding anything else to put in their place had shattered, falling at her feet in piles of dust. There was nothing more for her, nothing to look forward to, to hope for. She'd had her short taste of freedom and it was over. She had no possibility of avoiding her future any longer. So she would dress, and collect her last few belongings and when Karim returned he would find her waiting, if not ready, for the marriage that had been planned out for her when she was a child.

It was time to forget about dreams and to accept the future that fate and her father had decided for her.

CHAPTER EIGHT

ENGLAND WAS A lifetime away.

Three days. Thousands of miles. The other side of the world. And she felt as if she'd lived a whole lifetime since then.

Clemmie stood by the high window and stared out at Rhastaan city spread out below her at the foot of the hill on which the palace was built. If anything brought home to her how much her life had changed, then it was this city set on the outskirts of the desert, a heavy heat haze hovering on the horizon and a total lack of any wind to stir the flags on the royal buildings.

If she opened the window, then the ferocious heat of the day would rush into the room, fighting against the almost brutal air-conditioning that kept the place cool. Kept it liveable in. It was amazing just how quickly she had got used to a very different atmosphere, very different temperatures so that in spite of the fact that it was the sort of environment she'd grown up in, the raw heat of this desert kingdom was almost unbearable. She was actually longing for the cold of the little cottage that had been her home, her haven for such a short time. Here, she was surrounded by every comfort, every luxury, and yet she would trade it all in an instant for another few days of feeling free, of really being herself as she had been in Yorkshire.

But that was never going to happen.

With a deep, dragging sigh, Clemmie turned away from the window and moved back into her room, her bare feet making no sound on the pink veined marble tiles, the turquoise silk of her long robe sliding sensuously over their polished surface. Another thing that she would gladly go without if she could. The robe might be made from the finest silk, be decorated with beautiful embroidery and have been made exactly to her measurements but she longed for the battered jeans and tee shirts she had lived in before.

Clemmie plonked herself down on a padded stool and stared at her reflection in the dressing table mirror. She barely recognised herself, with her make-up done in a way she would never have chosen, heavy kohl outlining her eyes, rich red lipstick emphasising her mouth. And her hair…!

The wild dark locks had been pushed and pinned into an ornate arrangement of smooth, elaborate curls that pulled at her scalp and made her head itch. She was the woman her father had wanted her to be, trained her to be, but she couldn't help wondering what Karim, who had wanted her to look and behave like a future queen, would think of it.

Karim.

Just his name sounded alien inside her head. He had come into her life in a storm and had turned it upside down. For a few crazy, dangerous hours she had thought that he might be more than just the man who had been sent to collect her. That he could be something special. She couldn't have been more wrong.

If she had needed anything to drive that home to her, then the journey here would have been all that it would have taken. She might as well have been a piece of luggage that he had collected and had to deliver to Nabil, he had spared her so little attention. With her car out of the way, he had grabbed her small case, taking it out to dump it in his vehicle, then, opening the front passenger door, he had stood there waiting for her, not a word being spoken. When she had come past him to slide into her seat he had held himself stiff as a statue hewn from granite, keeping well back from touching her. Only his eyes had moved but when she had met his gaze it had been hard as polished jet and every bit as impenetrable.

Had he spoken more than one sentence to her?

'Seat belt…'

The command had been tossed at her as he'd climbed into the car beside her and put the key in the ignition. And then that had been it. Silence. When she'd tried to speak, he had just flicked a sidelong glance at her and then made a gesture to where the rain that had replaced the snow was lashing against the windscreen, reducing visibility to a minimum and making driving conditions very difficult.

'I need to concentrate.' It was clipped, blunt, totally dismissive. And then he had added, 'We need to get to the airport and on a plane to Rhastaan before Ankhara finds out where we are.'

If there was anything guaranteed to clamp her mouth shut, then it was that. How could she have forgotten about the man who was set against her marriage to Nabil? He was the head of a group who would do almost anything to make sure that the alliance that marriage represented never took place. Huddling into the raincoat she had pulled on over jeans and a jumper, she pulled her jacket tightly round her, chilled to the bone in a way that had little to do with the weather and was more the result of her thoughts.

Whatever else had happened between them, she needed Karim to get her to Rhastaan safely. He had been sent to protect her, and that was clearly what he was intent on doing—that and nothing more. She could do nothing but go along with him and do as she was told, for now.

It had been the same at the airport. Clemmie had been ushered from the car, through a bewildering series of gates and up into the private jet before she had fully registered just where they were. All formalities were dealt with by Karim, her luggage was loaded on board—and once she was settled in the plane, safely belted into her comfortable seat, it was Karim who disappeared into the cockpit to pilot them to Rhastaan himself. She hadn't seen him from the moment they had taken off until just before landing. Or, if he had come back into the cabin at any point, she hadn't been aware of it. Once in the air, and with her body finally feeling warm and something close to relaxed after the small meal and a hot drink prepared by an attentive stewardess, the stress of the past couple of days and the broken night had caught up with her and she'd fallen fast asleep. She'd only woken when the same stewardess had touched her shoulder to warn her to fasten herself in for landing.

'Madam…'

A careful cough, a quiet voice, drew her attention now to where Aliya, the maid who had been assigned to her on arrival at the palace, stood in the doorway.

'You have a visitor, madam—downstairs.'

Nabil. Who else could it be? She had been waiting for this summons ever since they had arrived at the palace.

In fact she had been surprised to find that her husband-to-be hadn't been at the airport to greet them, or at least arranged a meeting as soon as the sleek black car with the darkly tinted windows had swept up to the palace. She had nerved herself for it, determined not to show any weakness in front of Karim. He believed she had tried to run away from her responsibilities, that she was not fit to be a queen. So she would not let him see that she was afraid, or that she was concerned in any way. Head high, back straight, she had stalked into the palace, expecting to see Nabil.

And had only been met by his High Chamberlain.

Since then she had been alone in the palace apartment assigned to her. No one to talk to. No one to keep her company. Once from her window she had seen Nabil, walking in the courtyard.

He had been talking to a young woman, small, dark, very pretty, his head bent towards her, and he hadn't noticed Clemmie at her window, watching them. For a moment she had considered going out to speak to him but in the end had changed her mind. This relationship, this marriage had been forced on both of them when they were too young to do anything about it. It was best to leave things until Nabil was ready to come to her. But after that she had heard that he had left the capital, flying out to his summer palace. Obviously he was no keener than her to get this marriage underway.

So now, it seemed, the summons she had been expecting had finally arrived. Squaring her shoulders, she drew in a deep breath as she nodded to Aliya.

'I'm coming.'

The man who was waiting in the reception room on the ground floor was bigger than she had expected. Taller,

broader in every way than she might have anticipated of
a boy who had just had his eighteenth birthday. He was
standing as she had been minutes before, staring out of
the window, head slightly bent, one strong hand braced
against the wall. And it was that hand that gave him
away as she came nearer, recognising a gold signet ring
on the fourth finger.

'I... Karim?'

Had her heart really leapt up into her throat, pounding so hard that it seemed to have cut off her breathing,
making her pulse thunder in her ears?

He took his time about turning round, making her
feel that perhaps he had known she was there in spite
of the soundless steps that had taken her into the room,
closer to him.

'Clementina...'

The slight inclination of his dark head was the only
acknowledgement of her position here at this court. He
was a High Prince too, his attitude said, and as such he
wasn't going to bow to her. Which was fine with Clemmie. The truth was that she was already sick of all the
bowing and scraping she had received. It would have been
bad enough anyway, but after the months of freedom, of
living like an ordinary woman in her grandmother's cottage, it seemed even more over the top.

'Or should I say, Princess Clementina?'

'Oh, please don't!'

She was too busy taking in the sight of him standing
there, big and strong and even more gorgeous than before,
to think about holding her tongue and just let the words
escape. She had never seen Karim in traditional robes
before, the flowing white garment contrasting startlingly
with the bronze tones of his skin, the polished jet of his

eyes. He had discarded the headdress and the black silk of his hair gleamed in the shafts of sunlight that came in through the leaded windows.

She knew she had missed him, but she hadn't known how much until now he was here again, standing before her, tall and powerful and devastating. She felt like someone who had been starving and who had suddenly had an incredible feast placed before her so that she didn't know where to look first, what to enjoy most. How could two days' absence have felt so long? How could this man have become so central to her life in the space of less than a week? And how had she survived the past days with the huge hole in her life that he had left behind?

'I did ask you to call me Clemmie.'

'But that was in another time, another place.'

Another lifetime, his tone said, forcing her to remember how he had reacted to her naïve attempts at seduction, the way he had assiduously kept so distant from her. He had delivered his parcel, completed his mission and he was done...

So why was he here now?

'I have come to say goodbye.'

It was as if Karim had read her thoughts as he offered the flat-voiced explanation of his appearance here. If the truth was told, she had never imagined that she would see him again and just to have the chance to see his face, hear his voice was more than she had dreamed of. But...

'Goodbye?'

He should never have come, Karim acknowledged as he saw her huge eyes widen in shock and surprise. He had told himself that he wouldn't ever see her again. That it was so much better that way—the only way. He had made a vow to fulfil his father's debt of honour and deliver Clementina to Nabil, and he had done just that. His duty done, honour satisfied, he was free to leave and go back home. Back to take responsibilities from the shoulders of his ailing father, to take the reins of government of the country he had never thought he would come to rule.

'What else is there to say between us?'

His conscience gave a nasty twist when she saw the flinch she gave at his tone. She tried to hide it, of course, bringing her head up and meeting his eyes so defiantly that it was all he could do to bite back a smile. So the other Clementina, the wild, mutinous creature who had answered the door to him that first day at the cottage, was still there underneath this new version. The tall, elegant woman in turquoise silk, that wild hair tamed and sleeked into an ornate arrangement, who had stunned him into silence when he had turned to see her standing there.

It was the wild-haired, barefoot creature he'd first seen he remembered when awake. But it was that other Clementina, skin warm from the nest of blankets, silken hair spread out over his chest, the sound of her voice whispering his name in his ear who'd haunted his dreams. That memory made him toss and turn in restless hunger so that he had woken, bathed in sweat and with his heart racing, his body hard even from imagining her. Her choking cry of *'I want you...'* was always there inside his head, driving him to a feeling of near-madness as he tried to rid himself of it.

He had told himself that the only sane way to deal with this was to go, never looking back. To put her behind him and head home, to the life that was now his and that she could never be a part of. That was best—for both of them.

So why the hell had he found it impossible to leave without seeing her one last time? Why had he come here now, like this, like some fool of a naïve adolescent unable to tear himself away from the current object of his adoration? Because that was all she was, all she could ever be. Today's sexual fantasy. One he could easily replace with another willing, warm—and much less dangerous—woman in his bed.

No, that thought had been a mistake. The idea of any woman in his bed only reminded him of how it had felt to hold Clementina so close. To know she was warm and willing—and totally forbidden to him. It had almost torn him apart to say no to her then. It would destroy him to remember it over again.

'You are here, where you belong, with your future ahead of you. Your birthday will be very soon.'

'Four days.' It was only a whisper so that he had to lean forward to catch it then immediately cursed himself for doing so as a waft of some heady floral perfume, mixed dangerously with the clean ultra-feminine scent of her skin tantalised his senses and made his lower body ache in hungry response.

To conceal his reaction he nodded sharply, taking a much-needed step back and leaning against a high carved pillar.

'Your wedding will be arranged soon and your coronation immediately after that.'

'My destiny.'

It was stronger this time, infused with the defiance he had expected. But there was something else, something that stiffened her slender neck, brought that pretty chin up just a touch too high. There was a new sheen behind those thick, lustrous eyelashes, something that betrayed an emotion she was determined to hold back and not quite succeeding.

'I will be Queen of Rhastaan.'

'You will.'

It was strangely difficult to nod in response. His own neck seemed to have seized up, his head refusing to move. He had been forced up against the thing he didn't want to think of. The image of Clemmie—*Clementina*—as Nabil's wife. In Nabil's bed. That long sexy body entwined with the younger man's plumper frame, her mouth kissing him, her legs opening…

Hell and damnation—no! With a ruthless effort he forced his hands to uncurl from the fists into which they had clenched, knowing without looking that the crescent shapes of his nails would be etched into his palms from the pressure he'd exerted on them.

The memories of the Clemmie he had known were the ones he had to push aside—for good. If anything brought home to him why that was vital then this woman, the tall, regal creature whose ornate make-up had nothing like the impact of her fresh-faced beauty, was a statement without words of all that came between them.

Clemmie was the woman he wanted most in all the world. But she was not just any woman. And he was not just any man. What he wanted had no place at all in what must happen, no matter how it clawed at his soul to acknowledge it. The Clemmie of the cottage no longer existed. There was only the future queen of Rhastaan. *This* was the Princess Clementina he must turn his back on or bring his country and his family's reputation down lower than Razi had already taken it.

'And my part in all this is done. I heard this morning that Ankhara's man has been found and captured. He will not be able to interfere in anything ever again. And you will be in no further danger from him.'

'So you are free to go. To get back to your own life. I should thank you for bringing me here safely...'

Could her voice have any less life in it? Clemmie wondered. She couldn't find the strength to say anything more, or ease up on the rigid control she was imposing on herself. If she did then she feared she would break down, reveal the turmoil that was churning viciously inside her, maybe even risk saying the one thing she knew she should never say.

'Don't go...'

The words reverberated inside her skull, making her head go back in horror as she heard her own voice and realised that she had done exactly what she had told herself she must *not* do. She should have clamped her lips tight over the words but they had escaped and now that they were said she couldn't call them back.

'Don't...'

Could his eyes get any blacker, his face stiffen more into marble stillness? He was looking at her in such shock that she wished the ground would open at her feet and swallow her whole.

'Do not say such a thing.'

His hand had come up, flattening against his chest, just below the base of his strong throat. Underneath his fingers, hidden now by the fine white material of his robe, were the scars she had felt on his body, the marks that had marred the beautiful tanned skin. Skin she had once been able to touch, to kiss. But only once.

'You don't know what you're saying.'

'Oh, but I do.'

In for a penny, in for a pound. She'd told herself she must never say anything—but, now that she had, there was little point in holding back any more. They had no future. No hope of any time together. But they did at least have this. And she was going to snatch at her one chance of letting him know how she felt.

'I've missed you. So much.'

'I've been busy.'

What had she expected him to say? That he had missed her too? Stupid, stupid, stupid! A naïve fantasy— a child's dream.

'Busy with more of those duties that are so important to you?'

The dark frown that snapped his black brows together almost unnerved her. But she didn't care. She refused to let that icy stare freeze her into silence. If this was the last time she could spend with him—the last time she would see him—then she wasn't going to waste it in pretending to feel anything other than what was really in her heart.

'I hope they were fascinating—and fulfilling. Unlike our night together.'

That made the heavy eyelids drop down over the glittering eyes, narrowing them to just slits, the burn of his scrutiny gleaming behind the thick black lashes.

'We did not have a night together.'

His voice was thick with a rejection that burned like acid deep inside. But her memories—memories she had relived over and over since she had arrived in Rhastaan— gave her the strength to go on.

'We could have had.'

Violently he shook his head, swinging away from her, turning towards the door.

'You were unhappy—afraid. You had nightmares… and I comforted you.'

'And that was all you did?' Clemmie challenged.

'All…' It sounded as if it came from a strangled throat,

rough and raw, and that determined her that she was not going to let him get away with it.

'Liar,' she said softly, then, encouraged by the way he had frozen, absolutely still, she made herself go on. 'You are a liar,' she said more forcefully, 'and a coward not to admit it. I'm not afraid to say I wanted more.'

Had she overstepped the mark, pushed him to a point where he wouldn't take any more? She saw his long body stiffen, recognised with a clench of the nerves in her stomach, a twist to her heart, the small movement towards the door, away from her. A movement that he stilled then reversed only a moment later.

'I wanted more…' he conceded and it was only as she tasted the faint tang of blood on her tongue that Clemmie realised just how hard her teeth had been digging into her lower lip, breaking the skin under their sharpness.

'I wanted you,' she croaked. 'And you…'

The words died in her throat as he swung back to face her, the livid burn of his eyes stark and harsh against the tautness of his skin, the white marks that were drawn tight at his nose and mouth.

You wanted me…

She tried to say it. She opened her mouth, once, twice. Her lips moved but no sound came out. No words were needed. But then she looked into his eyes and what she saw there meant that the words didn't need to be said.

Not those at least. But there was something she had to say before she could let him go. He had to hear it and then she would see if he could still walk out of the door.

CHAPTER NINE

'You wanted me but it was more than that.'

'How could it be more? We were just a man and a woman…'

'We weren't *just* anything. Don't you believe that there must be one person who is truly special—one person who's meant for us, for however short a time? Someone we meet who changes our life, puts our existence on a new path once and for ever.'

She thought he wasn't going to respond. That his mouth and his whole being had frozen so that he had lost all ability, all need to say a word. Then suddenly he blinked hard, just once, shutting his thoughts off from her.

'No,' he said, cold and stark, totally ruthless. 'No, I don't believe such fanciful nonsense.'

'But your brother—he was going to be married. He must have loved… No?' She broke off as the violent shake of his head, the tight line of his mouth rejected everything she said.

'What has love got to do with it?' he said.

'It's usual…' Clemmie began then caught the way he was looking at her and backed down hastily. Karim nodded grimly.

'My brother's marriage was carefully arranged,
planned for the best, for the future, to bring together our
country and hers for their mutual benefit—like yours.'

It was stabbing, pointed, deliberately so.

'He knew it and so did she. They both knew their
duty.'

There was something behind those words, something
she couldn't interpret. There had been an unusual emphasis on that, *'They both knew their duty'*, even with
Karim's personal emphasis on duty and honour, that
scraped over nerves that seemed too close to the surface.
The memory of the look he had turned on her when she
had questioned his miscounting on the game of Snakes
and Ladders came back to haunt her so that she shifted
uneasily from one foot to the other and then back again.

'And his fiancée—what happened to her when your
brother died? What would have been her *duty* then?'

'And mine.' It was flat, toneless, as opaque as his eyes.

'And yours?'

She had a nasty creeping sensation that she knew what
he meant but she didn't want to accept it. But his reply
took away that faint hope.

'With my brother gone, I was the Crown Prince. I in-
herited everything—his title, his lands—his fiancée.'

'His…You would have married the woman who had
been engaged to your brother? She would have become
your wife?'

Why ever not? What else would I do? He didn't have
to say the words; they were there in the cold-eyed look
he turned on her.

'The marriage was arranged between the Princess of
Salahara and the Crown Prince of Markhazad. It didn't
matter who held the title.'

'So you…' Was this behind the way he had behaved in the cottage? Why he had held back, pushed her aside as if she was contaminating him. 'You're married?'

If his expression had been cold before, it was positively glacial now. She'd trampled in unawares, and the glare he turned on her sent a damp shiver crawling down her spine.

'I am not married. She would not have me.'

Was the woman mad? Clemmie had no idea what his brother had been like, but given the chance of having Karim as her husband—arranged marriage or not—what woman would be crazy enough to turn down the idea?

'I don't believe you. There had to be more to it than that.'

'There was.'

Well, she'd pushed for that answer, but did she really want to hear the rest of what he had to say? Her throat felt so tight and horribly dry that she couldn't have asked him to stop if she'd tried.

Karim stalked away from her, the beautiful white robe swirling around his taut frame, his dark gaze fixed on a point some distance beyond the window. A point that she was convinced he was not actually seeing.

'Meleya was promised to my brother almost from birth. Then, when she was eighteen, she came to live in the palace, to get to know him. Their marriage was arranged—a date fixed, but my brother was out of the palace a lot. He was restless, unsettled. One day I followed him. I saw him with another woman.'

Cold, stiff, deeply disapproving of the way his brother had behaved. Did this man have no gentler streak in him, no understanding of what the softer feelings might mean? Was there only *duty* and *honour* in his make-up?

'That was the day that Razi crashed his car,' he said.

Did Karim know how his hand had moved to his chest, to rub at the spot where the scars, barely healed by time, ridged his skin under the fine material of his robe? Clemmie didn't need reminding just how he had got the damage to his body.

'You tried to save him.' And, of course, to save the honour of his family.

'I tried to get them both out. I failed.'

Did he even realise who he was speaking to? His eyes still had that unfocused stare into the distance.

'She was a married woman—married to someone else.'

Clemmie's throat closed up, shutting off her breath so that she thought she was going to choke. No wonder he felt so strongly about these things. It was no surprise after seeing his brother die in such circumstances. The pain of loss must be like the scars on his body. Healed over but still there, still needing to be lived around.

'Meleya's father refused to let her marry anyone from my brother's family.'

And that would have been the final insult, the final realisation that his brother had damaged the honour of his family, so that even his arranged bride would turn away. Clemmie felt that she could see why Karim had felt obliged to come and fetch her, to fulfil the debt his father owed, to restore his family's honour in the eyes of his world.

Impulsively she moved forward, laid a hand on his arm.

'I'm sorry.'

Polished jet eyes dropped to where her hand rested against his, her fingers manicured now, nails polished and groomed in a way they had never been before. Then he lifted his gaze again, clashed with hers, and held.

She should move away, Clemmie told herself. Should take her hand from his arm and step back as far away as possible. If she was wise—if she was sensible…

But she didn't feel sensible. She didn't want to move away. Even when she saw his head move, angling slightly so that she knew what was coming. His eyes were fixed on her lips, so intent that she could almost taste him already, know the pressure of his mouth on hers. And she wanted it. Needed it like breathing.

It was her last chance. The last time. He had said that he had come here to say goodbye and she knew that nothing could possibly change that. How could the man who valued honour so much—and now she knew why—ever do anything else? This was the last time she would see him. The last time she would touch him. The last time she would…

She didn't know if she moved first or if it was Karim. She only knew that at some place, halfway between them, their lips met and clung, breath mingling, eyes closing the better to experience the sensations that were flaring through every nerve, every cell.

Her hands twisted in his, turning, clutching, clinging. Time evaporated, their surroundings disappearing into a buzzing haze. There was only her and this man who just by existing had taught her what it meant to be a woman. How it meant to feel as a woman. To know the wild and carnal force that was sexual need, sexual hunger. She didn't care what might come between them, what Karim might put between them, she only knew that what she wanted was right here and now, in this place and—her breath escaped in a choking cry as his arms closed round her, hauling her tight up against him.

Swinging her round, he almost slammed her up against the wall, the marble hard and cold against her spine, the turquoise silk little to no protection against its cold smoothness. She welcomed it. She needed it to keep her in reality, her feet on this planet. Everywhere else in her was fire and heat, a conflagration that pulsed with every beat of her heart.

She was crushed between him and the wall, feeling the hardness of his need pressed against her and, with an instinct as old as time, she moved, adjusted her position so that his erection was held in the cradle of her pelvis, as close as she could get to the hungry pulse low down in her own body.

'Clemen…' Karim began but because she feared what he might say in spite of the evidence of his body against hers, she reached up, laced her fingers in the dark, crisp hair and pulled his head down to meet hers, her mouth opening to his.

He tasted wonderful. He felt wonderful. The jet-black hair slid under her fingers, the strong bones of his skull hard against their tips. He smelt wonderful, the scent of his body enclosing her like incense, making her senses spin. She couldn't believe that it had only been a couple of days since she had been close to him like this. It felt like a lifetime since he had been in the cocoon of blankets and had held her close.

But she had wanted more then and she wanted more now. In fact, she'd had more then. She'd had the real closeness of skin on skin, the touch of his hands on her flesh.

And it still hadn't been enough.

It could never be enough. The hunger that had started then had only grown in the time in between. The yearning that had built with the thought that Karim had left, that he had gone out of her life was overwhelming, taking her over. He'd come to say goodbye and she couldn't let him go, couldn't end it now without knowing, without experiencing more. It was obvious that Nabil wasn't interested in her. He might be bound to her by law, by diplomacy, but he had yet to show any interest in her as a person.

Her future might be mapped out for her by others, dictated by treaties and politics, but there were still a few days before those treaties came into being, before she was actually twenty-three. And for the first time in her life she was in the arms of a man who made her heart pound, who heated her blood, and drove all rational thought from her mind. She wanted this. She wanted Karim. No one else could ever create this feeling inside her. This need. This hunger. She wasn't going to waste this excitement, this magic on anyone else.

His mouth was at the base of her throat, his teeth grazing the fine skin over her racing pulse, his lips hot on her skin as he muttered her name, thick and raw. But it was when his hand skimmed up over her body, making her breasts burn, her nipples sting, that she moaned her hunger aloud, wild and unrestrained. The fire between her legs was making her writhe against Karim's hard powerful form, heat and moisture flooding her with every touch, every kiss. He was tugging at the turquoise silk, wrenching it aside, ripping the fine fabric as he did so, the tearing sound telling her that his own control was lost as much as hers. He was oblivious to where he was, to the fact that there was only the door between them and the rest of the palace.

Between them and total exposure.

'We can't do this here…'

She pulled his head up again, muttered the words roughly against his lips, terrified not so much that anyone might hear but that he might try to speak, to deny what was between them. They only had today. Just a few short hours. Surely he would not deny her… He couldn't…

She wasn't going to give him the chance as she clamped her mouth against his, met the invasion of his tongue with the welcome of her own. Somehow, awkwardly, sideways, she edged him towards the secret inner stairway she had discovered only the previous day. The small staircase that was used by the royal family only, hidden from public view. With Karim's back against the wall this time, she urged him onwards, upwards, holding his head prisoner against hers with one hand while she let her other hand stroke over his straining body, touching, caressing, teasing, deliberately tormenting him so that he wouldn't be able to think, to have any hesitation. She caught his moans of response in her own mouth, tasting his breath and the hunger on it as she urged him up towards the door to her room, each step a near stumble of need and yearning as they climbed blind, somehow making it to the landing without mishap.

'Inside…'

Clemmie knew she sounded breathless but it wasn't the climb that had made her that way. She was burning with frustration as the long robes that Karim wore came between her demanding hands and the need to touch his skin, to feel the heat of his flesh.

'Clemmie…'

The door slammed back against the wall, the sound reverberating round the silent palace. Clemmie tensed, hearing Karim's shaken voice, fearful that it was now when he would say that this had to stop. She had barely survived his rejection once before. She didn't know if she could endure it over again.

But Karim's hands were on her arms as he whirled her into the room and kicked the door to behind them. The spinning motion carried them part way across the floor, heading almost to the huge silk-covered bed that stood on a small dais in the centre of the room.

Almost but not quite. Somehow Karim took hold of the crazy dance that had caught them up. He stopped the careering path across the marble floor, almost stumbled, almost lost his footing. Almost.

But then he had a hold of himself, and of Clemmie. With a hasty adjustment, he brought them both to a halt, holding her upright while her head still spun with disorientation and desperate need, the room swinging round her so that she would have fallen if it was not for that powerful grip on her arms, hard fingers digging into her flesh so that she could almost feel the bruises forming under the pressure.

'Stop!'

The single word was both a command and a threat, bringing her to a halt even more strongly than his hold on her. She blinked hard, trying to clear her eyes, to meet the powerful glare of his, and shivered as she saw herself reflected once more in the polished jet depths as she had been on the night in the cottage. A night that seemed like a lifetime away.

'Karim…'

He couldn't be doing this again, could he? He couldn't

be so cruel—so dishonest! Because to insist on her stopping now could only be a lie. It had to be, with the burn
of arousal scoring the knife-edges of his cheeks, the furious beat of his heart under the powerful ribcage. He was
still hard and hot against her so why the hell was he…?

'Karim…'

She wriggled frantically in his hold, managed to raise
her hands to his face, wincing as she felt the granite hardness of the muscles that tightened against her caress, the
furious jerk of his chin as he repelled her touch. Surely
this couldn't be happening, not when he had been the
one who had been kissing her, caressing her in the room
below.

'Karim—please…'

If he wouldn't let her touch him, then perhaps she
could reach him some other way. Her slippers had been
lost somewhere along the crazy journey up the stairs
so that she had to stand on tiptoe to reach, but somehow she managed to reach up and press a soft and, she
hoped, enticing kiss in the hard plane of his cheek. Her
mouth lingered just for a moment as the tang of his skin
burned against her tongue, the intensely personal flavour
of his skin scalding her senses. The moment was a sing-
ing delight and a terrible torment all in one as she felt
the hardness of him against her, her breasts crushed to
the rigidity of his chest, the thunder of his heart a physical sensation against them. The scent of his body surrounded her, enclosing her in a cloud of warm sensation,
and that taste on her lips…

'No!' Karim's voice was a rough animal growl in her
ear, the snarl of a savage cat that faced an intruder into
its territory. An alien, unwelcome intruder.

'But…'

'I said no!'

Suddenly the room was spinning round her again, more sickeningly this time. She wasn't aware of just what had happened, wasn't aware of anything at all until she hit the side of the bed, landing with a gasp of shock on the silken covers where he had flung her with force, away from him.

For a moment as she looked up into his eyes Karim looked as stunned as she felt, some wild force glazing his eyes, making them look like polished black glass. But then he blinked and the movement wiped away every trace of emotion.

'I do not want you,' he stated flatly.

But that was too much. She had felt the tension, the heat in his long body. She had known the taste and pressure of his kisses. Her body still burned and stung where his hands had moved over her skin, the pressure urgent with need.

'Liar,' she said softly, then repeated more strongly, conviction giving her voice added force. 'You are a liar and that is the most impossible untruth. You could at least be honest.'

Karim's proud head went back as if he had been slapped in the face, dark eyes narrowing violently. For a moment Clemmie thought that he was going to fling something at her, verbally if not physically, or at least that he was going to spin on his heel and stalk out of the room. But then he drew in a deep breath, his nostrils flaring as he did so, and nodded, slow and controlled. And it was the control that worried her.

'And what, precisely, would that achieve?'

It would mean so much to her. It would give her something to hold on to in the dark, arid future that lay ahead of her. It would leave her with one happy memory to know that one man—*this* man—had actually wanted her for her and not because of the money, the power, the treaties that came with her. He had wanted her solely because she excited him. Because she was a woman and he was a man.

But she couldn't say that. It would be like ripping her soul from her body and laying it out in front of him for him to scorn, or, even worse, to ignore completely.

'It would be the *honourable* thing,' she flung at him and knew a bittersweet sense of triumph as she saw the tiny, almost imperceptible twist to his beautiful mouth that told her dart had hit home.

'Oh, would it, Princess?' he questioned and her heart seemed to turn to ashes inside her.

Princess, he had said. And that single word put her right in her place, telling her exactly what he thought about her. He might be attracted to her physically, he might even hunger for her as much as she did him, but she was still just the 'mission' he had been sent on. The runaway bride he had been sent to collect. The would-be queen he had to ensure would reach the throne.

So that his honour could be satisfied.

'It would be honourable to take this situation and make it even worse than it is?'

Karim prowled closer to where she lay in the middle of the bed, the fine material of his robe whispering across the marble floor. Clemmie shifted restlessly, pushed herself up on to her knees to face him.

'I—don't understand.'

'You wanted honesty—well, here's honesty…'

Suddenly she didn't want him to say anything. That frankness she had wanted now seemed so dangerous, so threatening. Yet she had pushed him to say it and she couldn't find the words to stop him. But it was too late.

'I do want you.' Karim's black eyes burned down into her wide amber ones, searing right into her thoughts. 'I want you like hell. Never doubt it.'

His hand flashed out, caught hold of hers, held it for a moment against his body, his fingers flattening hers against the swollen heat of his erection under the fine material. Just for the space of a couple of jerky heartbeats but then he released her and took several steps back, away from her.

'I want you so much that it's tearing me to pieces not to have you. But what does that do for us?'

There was a hard band around her skull, across her forehead and digging into her temples and it was tightening with every heartbeat, twisting cruelly. What was that saying about being careful what you asked for? Karim had given her what she wanted—what she had thought she wanted. She had forced it from him. He had said the words she had claimed, to herself, she wanted to hear.

And all that it had done was to put an even greater distance between them.

'It... You know it was an arranged marriage. One I had no part in, no agreement given. I was just a child. My father sold me!'

'The agreement is still binding. You are here to become Nabil's Queen.'

But I don't want to be Nabil's anything! The words burned on the edge of her tongue but she knew the danger they would bring if she spoke them. It was bad enough to know that they were inside her head but if she heard them spoken aloud, between her and Karim, then there was never any going back. How had she managed to live her life, get this far, without ever really facing up to the nightmare that her future was going to be? She knew now why she had made herself keep so much to herself. She had known instinctively that if she had come out from the glass dome she had built around herself she would never be able to go through with this.

But Karim had walked into her life, shattered that glass dome beyond repair. He had forced her out of her seclusion and let the real world in, and, like the story of Pandora opening that box, there was no chance of ever getting anything back inside again. There wasn't even that one tiny little thing called Hope left to offer her anything.

'But not yet…' she said.

Clemmie uncoiled herself from the bed and pushed herself to her feet, needing to be able to look him in the eye, not stare up at him from where she was. His height already gave him too much of an advantage.

'The agreement between our countries—my official marriage to Nabil—is only legal when I am twenty-three.'

The flashing glare he turned on her warned her not to go on but she couldn't give in. She was fighting for her life.

'And Nabil doesn't care! He wasn't even here to welcome me and I saw him—with another girl.'

It wasn't really any evidence of anything, but Karim's reaction was. A faint flicker of something across his set features, in the darkness of his eyes, told her that he knew more about this than he was letting on. And that gave her the strength to carry on.

'He has to take me as his Queen—to accept me formally. Before then, I'm free—I can be with anyone else—with you. Like I was that night in the cottage.'

The memories were there at the back of his mind; she could read them in the way he veiled his eyes behind those long lashes, the tight set to his mouth. But he was not going to let them into his rational thoughts.

'You were never mine.' It was a cold, blank statement.

'I could have been!'

'No, you could not. You were not mine. You are Nabil's.'

'Nabil didn't own me. I was not his possession. He still doesn't.'

'You were forbidden. I was sent to bring you here because everyone—Nabil—my father—my country—trusted me. I will not betray their trust.'

'Because you are a man of honour.'

'You make it sound as if it's an insult.'

'Oh, no—'

'Then we are back where we started, I think.'

Karim pushed both his hands through the black silk of his hair and rubbed his palms over his face, closing his eyes off from her for a moment.

'Princess…' There was that word again, driving home what he wanted without anything else needing to be said. 'I came to say goodbye—that is the only thing that needs to be spoken between us.'

No… Please, no…

She tried to say it; opened her mouth, once, twice, but no sound would come out. Karim would not have listened either. That much was evident from the opaque look in his eyes, expressionless as a carved statue.

'So—goodbye.'

His bow was just a faint sketch of a movement, no feeling behind it. An inclination of the head, a swift turn and he was heading for the door, taking everything he had brought into her life with him. Surely he would not be able to walk away from her, turn his back on her. But it seemed that Karim was perfectly capable of doing just that.

How did she argue against that? What could she possibly put before him to make him stop, listen…change his mind?

'But I love you!'

CHAPTER TEN

SILENCE.

Total, shocking, frightening silence. Nothing more.
All that had changed was that Karim now stood stock-
still, the long line of his back turned against her, his head
held high, his eyes fixed straight ahead. Other than that
total stillness, he gave no indication of having heard her,
so would she have to say those words again?

She would if she needed to. Because as soon as she
had spoken them she had known how true they were.
How far she had come from their first meeting that had
brought her awakening, then knowledge of how it felt
to be a woman, to now—to this, when she knew how
to *love* as a woman, with all that a woman's heart was
capable of. And she knew that that woman's love was
strong enough to endure whatever the future held for her
if she could just have this one day, one night—one time
of loving Karim and creating memories to hold in her
heart when the arranged marriage closed round her and
imprisoned her for life.

'I...'

She'd opened her mouth to say it again but at last
Karim had moved. Slowly he turned to face her.

'You love me?'

Did he expect her to deny it? Did he *want* her to deny it? Was that what was behind that stony expression, the tightly drawn muscles? Whatever he thought, it was impossible to turn back now.

'Yes, I love you.'

It felt better, more right, every time she said it. This feeling had been growing silently and secretly like a seedling uncurling under the earth, ready to push the little green spike out into the sunshine. That spike was there now, out in the light, and she recognised it for what it was. And she was glad to see it. So grateful to know that at least she had experienced this feeling once in her life. She loved this man and she would never have to live out her days not knowing what this felt like.

'I love you.' She said it again because she wanted to and because it made her smile.

A smile that was not mirrored on Karim's set face.

'Why do you love me?'

What sort of a question was that? He had knocked her off her feet in the moment he had appeared on her doorstep and nothing had been the same ever since.

'Isn't it obvious? I love you for who you are. For your courage in trying to rescue your brother. Your loyalty to your father and your country.' That had sent him out on this mission when he could have delegated it to someone else. 'And your sense of honour. You couldn't even cheat in a game of Snakes and Ladders, for heaven's sake.'

Her laugh, already brittle, shattered into tiny pieces as she saw the look he gave her.

'Then you will understand why I do this.'

'Yes—no—'

Now she saw where he was going and a cruel hand

reached out to grip her heart, twist it brutally so that she gasped in pain.

'But you don't have to. I don't want you to!'

Dark brows snapped together in a dangerous frown.

'It is not what you *want*—or what I want. It is what must be. You are legally promised to Nabil.'

'But…' Clemmie's protest faded on her tongue as Karim held his hand up to silence her. But it was the look in his eyes that took the sound from her mouth.

'You say that you love me—so you must love me as I am. All of me.'

He paused, waited a nicely calculated moment to drive the words home.

'The man I am. My sense of honour.'

Her wounded heart had actually stopped beating. She could no longer breathe, and knew that every trace of blood must have faded from her cheeks, leaving them whiter than the pillows on her bed.

'No…' she moaned, so low that he must have had to strain to hear it. But she knew that, hear it or not, he understood what she was trying to say—and would refute it. 'Please, no…just once.'

Even as she said it, she knew that there was no 'just once'. *Just once* would break the moral code he lived by. It would bring them together and destroy them in the very same moment. But the alternative would break her heart.

There was no alternative.

'When…' It was all she could manage, knowing with a dreadful sense of inevitability just what the answer would be.

'Now.'

It would destroy him if he stayed, Karim admitted. He couldn't remain in her company any longer and not pull her down on to that bed and make love to her. Not do as she asked, as she so obviously wanted. Hell, she had offered herself on a plate. He wanted it too; so much that the hunger was tearing his guts apart, and he didn't know how he could walk to the door without looking back.

She was so damn gorgeous—temptation personified. But—*love*?

If anything had convinced him that he was right to do this the way he had to, then that word was right up there. He had no right to stay unless he could offer her love in return. Hellfire, he had no right to stay at all. She had been forbidden to him from the start, and she was forbidden to him now. The repercussions of acting on the carnal hunger he felt would have the equivalent effect of a nuclear explosion. He couldn't offer her any hope of anything else, so he had no right to stay when doing so would only destroy her future as well.

'If I don't do this then I can never be the man you love. I will be someone else entirely.'

She understood that all right. He watched her take it in, absorb it, and realise the deepest truth of what he was saying. She nodded silently, eyes huge in the pallor of her face. Something—pride, defiance, anger?—held the muscles in her jaw and chin tight, but those amber eyes were shadowed with something that it twisted his conscience brutally to see.

He didn't have the time, or the right to try to make this any gentler. Hard and sharp—and fast—was the only way to do this now.

'Goodbye, Princess.'

And then, to his horror, he saw that she was doing that thing with her mouth, digging her sharp white teeth into the soft flesh of her lower lip. It was impossible to stand by and watch it this last time. Without fully being aware of having acted, he moved across the room, his hand going under her chin—a chin he only just realised was quivering with the force of control she was imposing on it—as he lifted her face to his.

'Don't...'

With his thumb he pressed her mouth open slightly, easing her lip away from the worrying force of her teeth. But he had made two mistakes. The first was the worst. He had touched her and now he knew that he would live for ever with this feel of her flesh against his, the warm scent of her breath on his skin. And, this close up, he could see the betraying shimmer of her eyes. His own reflection blurred in that sheen. She couldn't make this any harder for him—but at least he could make it as easy as possible for her. He could get out of here now, fast, and leave her to get on with her life.

But he couldn't go without one last kiss.

His first kiss was meant to be firm and fast. Just dropped on to her forehead. An unemotional, uninvolved farewell. But the minute his lips touched her skin he knew that would not be enough. Every male sense he possessed demanded more.

With gentle fingers under her chin, he lifted her face again and bent his head. The last kiss was softer, lingered longer, put all the hunger he felt into its pressure on her mouth. So much so that he felt he was getting dragged into a storm of sensuality that threatened to close over his head and drown him.

With an effort that tore at his being, he wrenched himself away.

'Goodbye, Clemmie.'

It physically hurt to walk towards the door. His body

screamed in angry protest but he forced himself to ignore it. This time he was going. He was not looking back. He was *not*…

It was only when he was out of the room and in the corridor beyond that he realised he had been holding his breath all the time so that he had to let it go in one great wrenching, gasping, brutal rush. The door closed behind him so that at last he was unobserved, and, taking a moment or two to find a way of breathing again, he forced himself forward. He got himself out of the palace the only way he could. By putting one foot in front of the other and never looking back.

Clemmie watched the door close behind Karim with eyes that burned cruelly, aching and dry. The tears that had been so close had vanished now. She couldn't let herself cry. She wouldn't let herself. She had told Karim that she loved him and he had still walked out on her. He had turned and walked out of the door, never once looking back.

And the real problem was that she understood perfectly why he had done that.

She had just let the man she loved walk out of her life. She couldn't do anything else. He was so right about that. If he had stayed, if he had taken what she offered, then he would not have been the man she had fallen in love with. She had lost her heart to a man of honour, never thinking of having that code of honour turned against her in a way that had ripped the soul from her body.

She loved him but she hated him for being so right about that. She couldn't fault his reasons for behaving as he had, however much she wished he had never done so. She could argue with anyone, with herself—but she couldn't argue with him.

She couldn't argue with Karim.

Her hand crept up to her mouth, her fingers pressing on her lips to hold the memory of his kiss for as long as she could possibly manage. Already the moisture from his mouth was drying, but she could still taste the essence of him on her lips. If she could have found a way to call him back, to see a way out of this, then she would have done.

But the truth was that there was no way out. She could not call him back without destroying the man he was. The man she loved for his integrity. He would not be the man of honour—if he had stayed—and how could she hate him for being such a man, even if it had destroyed her one chance at happiness?

She had thought once before that she had had to face the fate that lay ahead of her with a heavy heart and a sense of dread. But now that future seemed so much darker, so much bleaker because she had had just a taste, just a glimpse of how wonderful the alternative might have been.

An alternative that was now closed to her for ever.

CHAPTER ELEVEN

'HE HAS DONE *what*?'

Karim could not believe what he had just heard. He recognised the words but they just did not make any sense. Or, rather, they did make sense but not one he dared to put his trust in.

'Nabil has renounced her—revoked the marriage agreement,' his father stated again, holding out the sheet of paper he had been reading from. Karim snatched it, stared at it, but the words danced before his eyes.

'It is his right,' his father said calmly. 'It was always part of the treaty agreement.'

His right, maybe…but why? The words stilled, settled, and at last he could read…

'He has renounced her…' he echoed his father's words in a very different tone, his voice thick with the implications of this for Clementina, for Rhastaan—for him. 'But why?'

The rest of the message made things clearer in one way—but so much more confusing in another. His father might not recognise it, but there could be no doubt in Karim's mind just who was behind this.

It seemed that under interrogation Adnan—the ex-security man who had been in Ankhara's pay—had told

Nabil of the night that Karim and Clemmie had spent together alone in the cottage. A night that her prospective fiancée and everyone at his court had put a very different—a damning—interpretation on instead of the real one. No names were mentioned in the report his father had received, but Karim knew only too well who was the man involved. His conscience twisted at the thought.

But still things didn't make sense. No matter what accusations had been thrown at her, all Clemmie had had to do was to tell the truth. That nothing had happened. Why had she not said anything, flung Nabil's accusations in his face?

'It was Nabil's right—Nabil's decision,' his father was saying now. The older man's face had so much more colour now and his strength was improving daily. 'Our part in this is over. You fulfilled my vow to the boy's father. Honour is satisfied.'

Honour is satisfied.

The words that should have meant so much now rang hollow in Karim's thoughts. Honour might be satisfied, but he was not. How could he be when every day since he had come back from Rhastaan seemed shadowed, hollow—empty?

But I love you! Clemmie's impassioned cry echoed in his thoughts, taking him back to the terrible day in Nabil's palace when he had felt as if he was being torn in half as he had had to walk away from her.

Because she was Nabil's promised bride: the prospective Queen of Rhastaan. Which she was no longer.

The sound inside his head was so loud that he was stunned his father hadn't actually heard it. It was deafening enough to make his head reel, his thoughts spin.

It was the sound of chains dropping away, falling to

the floor. The chains that had bound both him and Clemmie. Tying them into a situation where they could have no hope of ever being true to themselves.

Of ever being just a man and a woman.

Once again he was back in Nabil's palace, recalling how he had looked at Clemmie, decked out in the silken robe, the ornate hairstyle, the elaborate make-up that marked her out as the promised Queen of Rhastaan. The woman who was forbidden to him.

No longer.

All that had been stripped away. She was no longer Princess Clementina, but just Clemmie Savanevski. Then he had wished that she was no princess, but just a woman—as she was now.

And in these circumstances, he was just a man. The man that Clemmie had enchanted from the moment he had first met her, and whose absence had darkened and frustrated his existence ever since.

And as just a man and a woman, was it possible that they could begin again?

'Happy Birthday to you! Happy Birthday to you!'

The chirpy refrain ran through Clemmie's head over and over, its bright, cheerful sound totally at odds with her mood.

Today was her twenty-third birthday, but there were no festivities, nothing in the world she felt at all like celebrating. Her life was so totally different from the way she had thought it would be. The path she had thought she was to take was now closed to her and she had no real idea of where she would go. She felt lost and unsure, and so cold!

With a shiver she wrapped her arms around herself,

pacing around the room in an attempt to warm herself when even the fire she'd lit didn't seem to have enough heat to take the bite out of the air. Was it just because she had become accustomed to living in the heat of the desert—for a short while at least—so that she felt the cold more than before? Or was it the truth that the chill came more from inside, from her heart, rather than the wintry weather?

It was all so very different from the day just forty-eight hours before, when she had been summoned to the throne room to meet with Nabil at last.

Clemmie sighed and moved aside the curtains at the window, staring out at the icy rain that lashed against the glass. The sun had been high and fierce in Rhastaan then and it was probably still shining down on Nabil and his new princess. The girl he had wanted all the time to take as his bride. The girl he had cast her aside for.

The morning had been like any other since arriving at the palace. Her breakfast tray had been brought to her, clothes laid out for her—a long silken dress in fuchsia pink. Her maid had been as attentive as ever, her eyes down bent, her attitude totally respectful. If there had been anything in the air, something to warn her of what was coming, she hadn't noticed it. But then she had been so down, her spirits so very low after the way that Karim had walked out on her two nights before, that she had gone through her dressing, the styling of her hair, the application of the ornate make-up, like an automaton. There had to be some way out of this but for the life of her she couldn't think of one.

In the end it was Nabil himself who had come up with the escape clause. And not in the way she had anticipated.

The sound of footsteps coming down the stairs had her

swinging round from the window, plastering the necessary smile on to her face as a small, dark-haired bundle
of energy came thundering into the room, followed more
sedately by his mother.

'Clemmie!' Harry flung himself into her welcoming
arms, enveloping her in a huge hug. ''appy birfday!'

'Do you think he'll ever get tired of saying it?' she
asked Mary as their eyes met over the top of the dark,
shining head.

'I doubt it,' her friend laughed. 'After all, this is the
first year he's had a big sister to wish a happy birthday to.'

'Well, I hope there will be dozens and dozens more.'
With an effort she managed to smooth out the shake in
her voice, that smile a little less fixed and forced now.
'After all, it looks like this will be my home from now
on.'

'Such a tiny place after what you could have had.'
Mary's gaze went round the small shabby room. 'When
I think of what you've had taken from you.'

'Oh, no,' Clemmie hastened to reassure her. 'What
was taken from me? A marriage I didn't want. To a man
I didn't love and who didn't want me. A kingdom I could
never have belonged in.'

On the positive side, she'd gained her freedom from
her father's tyrannical rule and now had the chance to
develop a real relationship with her adored little brother.

'True enough.' Mary nodded, picking up Harry's coat
in preparation for the journey home. 'Looked at that way,
you didn't really lose so very much after all.'

Mary had to say that, Clemmie admitted to herself.
Because she hadn't been told the whole story. So she
knew nothing about the real loss she'd endured in all this.
The emptiness that tore at her heart. The loss of the man

she had fallen headlong in love with. Fallen so deeply and so completely that now her life felt as if it had a gaping, raw hole right at the centre of it.

'And even the peace treaty managed to work out in the end—after some heavy-duty diplomacy.'

'But only because you let Nabil get away with everything he wanted. You could have put up more of a fight; told him how wrong he'd got everything.'

Clemmie felt a chill slide down her spine as her friend's words made her remember her last day in the palace at Rhastaan, the accusations that Nabil had flung at her.

'I didn't want to fight—and what good would it have done?'

The only fight she'd had in her had been to declare the truth. And that would have made matters so much worse.

'But he threw you out. Now even your own father won't have you back. You told me what he said.' Mary shook her head, her eyes darkened with concern for her friend.

'"You are tainted—what man will want you now?"' Clemmie echoed her father's dismissive response.

'I will.' The voice came from behind her. From where the battered wooden door had opened silently, allowing a man to come into the room.

A man. *The man.* The man she had thought that she would never ever see again.

A man who seemed taller, darker, more dangerous than he had ever been before. She had met this man here when he had come for her. He had taken her back to Rhastaan because he had been given the task by his father and because his honour demanded that he carried out that debt which his family owed to Nabil. He had handed her over…

And then he had walked away from her because, in spite of the fact that he admitted he wanted her, hungered for her more than he could bear, his damned *honour* demanded that he did so.

She had told him that she loved him; that she wanted him as much as he wanted her and he had still walked away.

Now Karim was back in her life and she had no idea why he was here or what his plans might be.

'Karim…' It was just a breath, a whisper of reaction.

'Clementina.'

There was much more strength in his response but his voice was rough and uneven as if it was fraying at the edges. He barely looked around the room, taking no notice of Mary and the little boy who was gaping at this new arrival in frank curiosity.

He was hardly dressed for the cruel weather outside. A supple leather jacket, a tee shirt that was so wet from the rain that the dark curls on his chest showed through the white material. The black silky hair was plastered to the fine bones of his skull, his bronzed skin slick with the rain so that his high cheekbones looked sharp as knives. But it was the burn of the dark eyes above them that caught and held her, stopping the breath in her lungs.

Those black eyes were fixed on her face, his stare so intent it burned away the topmost protective layers of skin, leaving her raw and exposed underneath. Her own gaze was caught and held, mesmerised, unable to look away, trapped into immobility no matter how wildly her mind screamed at her to break away. To run.

But to run from him or to him? She had no idea and her brain couldn't compute any possible answer.

'Clemmie…' Mary tried for her attention, her tone making it plain that she knew there was little chance of her being noticed. 'I think I should go. Harry—come here—get your coat on.'

Something in the thickening atmosphere in the room had communicated itself to the little boy and he made no protest, didn't even resist when his mother bundled him into his coat, then grabbed for her own jacket. And still the connection between Clemmie and Karim was locked, absorbed, almost a physical thing, a spider's web of connection, so fine and yet impossible to break.

'Call me…'

Mary was bustling Harry out of the room, but she turned for a moment in the doorway to glare both at Karim and then at Clemmie, but in such very different ways.

'If you need me…'

'She will.'

Karim might have been speaking to the air; not the slightest turn of his head acknowledged Mary's presence behind him. And Clemmie could only bring herself to dip her head in agreement, unable to drag her eyes away from the man before her.

The slam of the door behind her friend and Harry made her blink once, hard. But when she looked again *he* was still there.

'What are you doing here?' She forced the words out, hearing them crack in the middle.

Not even the flicker of a smile warmed his face.

'You know why I'm here,' he said harshly. 'I've come for you.'

The words he had used the first time he had come here. On the day that he had appeared at the door of the cottage. Then he had taken her life, her heart, into those powerful hands of his and turned them inside out.

So *was* she crazy to feel so glad to see him? She didn't know, didn't care, only knew that her heart had leapt at the sight of him and that she was glad for the chance to spend a few more hours in his company. A few more hours when her eyes could linger on the dark strength of his face. When she could hear his voice. When the hunger that had haunted her nights, made her toss and turn, waking in sweat-soaked sheets, now had physical form. And he was only metres away from her.

'How do we do this?'

Was he feeling anything like the way she was? Had the same yearning she was feeling put that rough laughter into his voice? Was there really just a shabby rug on the floor between them or had an enormous chasm opened up at their feet that she didn't know how to cross to reach him?

Suddenly Karim flung his arms open wide, stretching the white tee shirt tight across his chest, his eyes burning into hers.

'Hell and damnation, Clementina, we can do this now. Come here. Come to me before I go crazy with wanting you.'

She wanted it too. She wanted his arms around her so much but in the same breath her mind was warning her, telling her that she knew nothing of his reasons for being here. Nothing except that he had come for her. She took one hesitant step forward and then it was as if just the movement had broken the spell that held her frozen.

One more step—and then another. And then she was

running—flying it felt like—over the floor to where he stood waiting for her, those powerful arms still outstretched.

He was moving too, rushing towards her so that they met—collided—with such force that Clemmie lost her footing, stumbled, fell, taking Karim with her. She landed on the settee, the breath driven from her lungs as the weight of Karim's body crushed her, her gasp of surprise snatched from her lips as his mouth took hers. The taste of him went straight to her head like the most potent fiery spirit, intoxicating her in a second. It was all she wanted but it was not enough. How could it ever be enough when this was what she needed, what she'd longed for? She'd only been apart from him for a few days but those days had left her starved, desperate for this. In the moment that he lifted his body slightly she thought he might move away from her and grabbed at his shoulders, at his head, clenching desperate fingers in the crisp darkness of his hair to hold him still, close to her.

'No… Don't leave me…' It was a yearning cry and she felt rather than heard the laughter that shook his long body.

'No,' he muttered, rough against her lips. 'Definitely no. I have travelled halfway across the world for this. I have no intention of giving up now.'

He had only moved to pull her underneath him so that the heat and weight of his body pressed her into the scattered cushions of the sofa. He was almost crushing the breath out of her but she welcomed the heated imprisonment, knowing that this was what she had been dreaming of at nights, what she had been longing for through the days.

His mouth was on hers, his tongue seeking hers, tast-

ing her, inviting her, provoking her. She followed his lead
so gladly, her head spinning with the joy of it, the sensual
force of his kisses making her mind blow apart. The wet
tee shirt was damp against her face but she didn't care. It
brought home to her that this was no fantasy, no figment
of her imagination. It was real—it was true. He was here,
with her and this was actually happening.

He tasted wonderful. He smelled wonderful. He felt
wonderful. He was all male and everything about her
that was female was responding to his touch on her skin,
his fingers tangling in her hair. His hands were everywhere, touching, caressing, enticing, demanding. When
he curved them over her breasts, cupping her through
the soft wool of her sweater, she arched her back up to
meet the caress, pressing herself against his touch. Needing more.

Her own hands were scrabbling at his clothes, tugging the leather jacket off and discarding it somewhere
on the floor. The tee shirt followed it, tangling crazily,
wildly with her own sweater as he pulled it off to allow
him freer access to the curves of her breasts pushing
against the pink silk of her bra. A moment later that too
had joined the growing bundle of their clothes on the
floor and Clemmie's breath hissed in between her teeth
as skin burned against skin and she felt she would pass
out from the pleasure the intimate friction brought her.

His mouth was at her breast now, suckling her, deli-
cately at first, then harder, deeper, stronger. Drawing her
distended nipple deep into his mouth and scraping his
teeth gently over it so that she moaned aloud in uncontrolled response.

'More…more…'

She panted it from between dry lips, her body writhing under his, knowing what she wanted and yet not daring to believe that it might actually be within her grasp. That she might actually know the truth of this man's possession.

'There will be more—I promise,' Karim assured her, thick-voiced. 'I've waited—and wanted—and now I've come to take my reward—and to give you all that you need. Like this...'

Another set of heated kisses were pressed against her other breast, licking it, nibbling at it until it was burning in sensation like the first.

'And this...'

That wicked mouth moved lower, sliding down over her skin, kissing its way to where the waistband of her jeans was an unwanted barrier. Clemmie's breath caught in her throat as she waited, frozen, yearning, needing...

He paused for just a moment, tracing the line of her belt with the warmth of his tongue, and then he flicked open the buckle, slid down the zip, following the line of pale skin that he had exposed with yet more kisses as he tugged the soft denim from her hips.

'Yes—oh, yes.'

Her hands tangled in the dark hair, holding him tight against her while her most intimate core pulsed in hungry anticipation, needing more, needing it now—and yet not wanting to lose a minute of every wonderful sensation he was creating in her. Bolder than she had ever anticipated being, she found the fastening of his jeans, tugging them open, fighting to push them off. Karim helped her, lifting his hips so that the material slipped down his legs, kicking them off the edge of the sofa before he came to settle, warm and strong, and so very powerful, between her opening thighs.

She was naked to him now. Naked and open and so very willing. The fear she might have thought would intervene, making her pause and hesitate, didn't strike at all. Instead it was Karim who paused, drawing in a deep ragged breath, and he looked down into her eyes, searching for what he needed in her face.

'This is your first time…' The rough growl of his voice told him how hard he was finding it to keep his control for long enough to ask the question. 'Are you…?'

'Yes.' Her kiss, hot, hungry, passionate, closed off the question he had been about to ask. He didn't need to ask but she still had to reassure him, couldn't let him wonder, doubt for a minute that this was what she wanted. 'I couldn't be any surer—I've waited so long—too long!'

The last word was a cry of shock and delight as, not needing any further encouragement, Karim yielded to the hungry force that was pulsing through him and eased himself inside her, sliding deep surprisingly easily where she was slick and moist with wanting him.

'All right?' he breathed, raw and uneven, and she couldn't find a word to answer him. She could only nod again and again, pushing herself against him, opening up to him, drawing him in.

'Yes…' she managed as he shifted his weight, pressed harder, further.

Just for a moment there was a burning pain, a stinging discomfort that had her gasping, fingers digging into the hard naked shoulders above her, eyes open wide. For a couple of heartbeats she froze, waiting until the burn had subsided, but then she relaxed back against him, moving her hips to encourage him, slowly, tentatively at first then more confidently, faster, meeting every powerful thrust of his strong body into hers.

You're mine.

The words sang inside her head as she gave herself up to the sensations that took over her body, loving the way they were building up, reaching for something just out of reach, something so wonderful she didn't dare to begin to imagine it.

You're mine and I'm yours—yours—*yours*...

And then there was no possibility of words, or thoughts, only feelings and wonder. Whatever had been out of reach was now rushing towards her, wild and glorious and out of this world. She opened herself up to it and let it take her, let him push her right over the edge into a brilliant and explosive world where there was nothing but herself and Karim and the sensations that they had created between them.

CHAPTER TWELVE

THE NIGHT HAD slipped away from them, burned up in heat and hunger and wonderful, glorious fulfilment. At some point exhaustion had claimed them and they had dropped into sleep that had swamped them totally, keeping them unconscious until outside, beyond the window, the late winter sun finally began to rise.

Fingers of light crept under Clemmie's closed lids, bringing her awake, and slowly, gingerly she stirred, easing herself up from the nest of blankets they had built around them at some point in the darkness of the night. With a smile that recalled the delights of their lovemaking she looked down at where Karim's dark head rested against the crumpled pillows, one arm flung up beside it.

Karim. Her lover and her love. The man who had made her his so completely through the night.

In the new light the scars on his chest looked raw and angry, making her heart clench at the thought of him being hurt so badly. And at remembering that he had got them trying—but failing—to rescue his brother. With gentle fingertips she traced the brutal lines, smoothing a soft caress over them. She heard his breath hiss in between his teeth and lifted her head to look into those black, watchful eyes.

'Did I hurt you? I'm sorry...'

'No.'

He caught her chin in firm but gentle fingers, holding her still when she would have turned away, bringing his head down so very close to hers that she could feel the warmth of his breath on her skin.

'No,' he said again, deeper, rougher as his gaze seared her. 'You caused me no pain. But I was surprised. Soraya hated the scars.'

She knew there had been other women before her but still it gave her heart a twist to hear her name.

'But why? They were won in honour.'

The word fell into a pool of silence, making her world tilt sharply just once, then back again but to a point where she felt she no longer had a sense of balance. She had been so happy to see him reappear in her life that she hadn't been able to think before she had flung herself into his arms. His touch had been like putting a flame to the blue touchpaper on an explosive, instantly devastating, destroying any hope of thinking rationally. She had given herself to him again and again without a care for her own safety or the protection of her heart. But now she could think and those unwanted thoughts reminded her that she had no idea at all what, other than the lust that had so clearly driven him, had brought him here.

I have travelled halfway across the world for this, he had said. But could he have travelled so very far *only* for that? No matter how powerfully he had wanted her, was that enough?

Because he *had* wanted her. How could she ever doubt that when her body still sang with the after-effects of the fulfilment she had known, parts of her aching, the delicate inner tissues bruised in a way she welcomed as the proof of her initiation into womanhood. The evidence of a man's—*this* man's—need of her, the hunger that his body had felt for hers. And hers for him.

But he had felt that before and because she had been promised to someone else his honour had kept him from acting on it. Now she was no longer forbidden, they were both free...

Free to do what?

Free to do what they wanted. She knew that *this*—the heated passion they had just shared—was what Karim had wanted all along. He had never offered her anything else. But she had longed for more. If he had nothing more to give her then she would have to find the strength to be content with what he offered.

Uncomfortable and restless, she eased her chin free of Karim's grasp and wriggled upright, pulling one of the blankets with her and clutching it to her breasts as she stared into the glowing embers of the fire. The heat scorched her eyes but the burn was nothing compared with the sting of unshed tears that pushed at the back of them.

'Clemmie...?'

She felt Karim move behind her, the sudden rush of cooler air as he eased away from her, propping himself up against the arm of the settee.

'What is it?'

'Nothing.'

It was just a mutter, low and gruff, and she wouldn't have believed herself either, so she wasn't surprised when she heard Karim's response.

'Liar!'

There was a touch of laughter in the half-amused re-proach. But it was the other half of his tone that stabbed and twisted deep in her soul. A blunt fingertip touched at the back of her neck then slid gently down her spine. The gentle caress made her shiver as it stirred once again the hungry physical responses she might have thought were at least dormant for a while. But it seemed they were still there, just below the surface, waking at just a touch, and threatening to swamp her mind.

And she needed to think.

'Don't!'

She flinched away from his touch rather more violently than she had intended. The gentle touch was like the scrape of thorns with her nerves so very near the surface. She knew the mistake she had made when she sensed the tension in the powerful body behind her, the freezing of the movement of his hand.

'What is it?' Karim asked, his tone putting an edge on the question. 'Did I hurt you? Is that it?'

'No. Of course you didn't hurt me.'

At least, not in the way he meant. He had been a wonderful lover, careful, considerate, gentle when she had needed him to be so, and responsive enough to recognise when gentleness was the last thing she wanted.

'I mean—well, of course it was bound to be a little—difficult at first—but that was all. I wanted you. I wanted this.'

There was silence behind her as he absorbed that. He would not be satisfied, she knew, and the nerves in her stomach twisted into painful knots as she waited for what would come next.

'Then what is it? What is it you are not telling me...? Look at me!'

It was a command she didn't dare to disobey. If she turned she feared that he would see the truth that must be written on her face. But if she didn't then he would know something was up—and he wouldn't give her any peace until he found out what it was. Five days ago, in despair, she had told him that she loved him and had had to watch as he turned his back and walked away from her. She didn't think she could cope with risking that happening again.

'I'm sorry…' Dragging up the strength from somewhere deep inside, she turned to face him, flashing a smile that she hoped was convincing. 'I was just—trying to absorb all that has happened.'

If she looked into his eyes she would be unable to go on so she forced herself to focus on the dark hairs on his chest, watching them rise and fall with each breath he took. His breathing was deep and regular, quite unlike her own tight, shallow gasps.

'After all, it's not even a fortnight since I was here, packing, knowing that my birthday—and my wedding— was just days away. And then you appeared at my door.'

Had there been a tiny jolt in the regular, even beat of his heart? She could have sworn that just for a second something had made him react.

'And then you disappeared out of the window—to see that little boy?'

When he had first arrived, Karim recalled, the small boy had been hugging her tight. As soon as he had appeared, her friend had bundled the child into his coat and left with him hastily. But not before he had caught sight of the small sturdy body, the dark hair, the face that had been an almost mirror image of the one that was now in front of him. The shock that was clear on Clemmie's face told him he was right.

'She called him Harry,' he said quietly. 'And the first

day you tried to get extra time—to go and see someone—
you began to say his name then cut it off.'

He didn't need her to give any response. It was there
in her eyes, in the film of tears that caught the firelight
and multiplied it.

'He is your brother?'

Clemmie's head moved slowly in a nod of acknowledgement.

'My mother ran from my father when she realised she
was pregnant.' Her voice was low and hesitant, but it grew
in confidence as she told her story. 'She was terrified that
this child would be taken and—sold—into marriage as I
had been, and she was determined that nothing like that
would happen to this new baby. She knew she was already ill, so she gave him up for adoption and sadly she
died very soon after he was born.'

'So this is why you came here, to look for him?'

She'd come to trace her one other family member not,
as her reputation had declared, just to have some time of
freedom, some fun, before she married.

'Yes. I found out about him when I learned that Mother
had come here, to Nan's cottage, before she died. She
left me a note that told me who had adopted Harry and I
just had to see him, if only once. But I couldn't tell anyone about him.'

Karim felt the shudder that shook her slender body as
a reproach without words. Intent on fulfilling his duty,
locked into that code of honour, he hadn't spared enough
thought for the effect it had had on her, the prospect of her
life being taken away from her. Arranged marriages were
so common in his world. It was only when he had come
up against this one that he had been made to reconsider.

'If my father had known, he wouldn't have hesitated to take him back—to use him for his own ends.'

'He will never learn of him from me.' Karim reached out and covered her shaking hands with his own, looking deep into her eyes. 'You are under my protection now. Your father will never touch you again.'

Her laughter was shaken, right to the core. There wasn't even a trace of humour left in it.

'He wouldn't want me. He'll be happy if he never sees me again. Nabil has discarded me and now, as far as my father is concerned, my reputation is ruined. I bring the shadow of that scandal with me.'

Black cold fury sliced through Karim like a blade of ice and he reached out to pull her close, her head resting against his chest where his heart thudded in anger. As soon as skin touched skin he felt the bite of sexual need as it flooded his body, but he had to clamp down hard on it, fighting a brutal battle with the desire that threatened to destroy his ability to think.

For now he had to think. He had to know.

'If I had realised that Ankhara's man had known about our night together...'

The dark head that rested over his heart stirred slightly, and he felt the new tension in her body.

'We weren't *together*.'

Not for her want of trying. And now, with the scent of her skin around him, the softness of her flesh against his hands, he didn't know how he had managed to hold back, how he had ever been able to deny himself this pleasure, this satisfaction. But could it ever be more than that?

'Why didn't you tell Nabil that you were still innocent? That nothing had happened?'

'And he'd have believed that?'

She hadn't been mistaken then, Clemmie realised. The steady pulse under her cheek had definitely missed a beat. Held this close, this tight, she couldn't be unaware that he was as hot and hard and ready for her as if they had never made love at all that night. Her own senses were responding to that knowledge, her body softening, moisture dewing the folds between her legs as an answering beat set up in her blood in response to the pound of Karim's heart.

All she would have to do was to turn closer in to him. To lift her face and press her mouth against his, smooth her hands down over the powerful ribcage, towards the thrust of his erection under the blankets. She could entice him into lovemaking and this awkward, difficult conversation would never have to be. She would never have to risk hearing him say that she had done it all for nothing. That she had played hazard with her future, her reputation, to get out of the contract that bound her to Nabil for only a few nights of heated passion. A blazing sexual affair that was going nowhere.

'How could I tell him that when it would have been a lie? When he had only to look into my face—into my eyes—to know.'

Because something *had* happened. Something that had changed her life, changed her entirely. After that one night with Karim she could never be the same woman ever again. And it hadn't been sex that had changed it, though it might just as well have been. If he had made love to her then he couldn't have changed her any more than he had just by being himself.

By being the man she had fallen in love with.

She had been deluding herself to think that she could ever go through with the arranged marriage that had been set up for her. She had been sleepwalking towards a fate that she had no idea how it really was, how it would really feel. She had never really known what feelings were possible in a female heart, just what was possible between a man and a woman. What being in love truly meant and how shockingly powerful the feelings could be.

'Something had happened. And I couldn't pretend that it hadn't.'

Something as earth-shattering, as elementally powerful as a volcano exploding and spewing red-hot lava into the atmosphere. It had changed her for ever and she had known that there was no hiding it, no pretending from here on in.

'I told him that I was no longer the woman he thought I was—that I could never be the wife he wanted.'

She tried for a raw, jerky laugh of irony, only to find that it cracked and broke in the middle.

'It turned out that I wasn't the wife he wanted at all, anyway. He was only too grateful to me because he had been looking for an excuse not to go ahead with our marriage—but to marry Shamila instead. Apparently she's already pregnant with his child.'

The deep sigh that Karim drew in lifted her head but then she let it drop again. She knew that the only way she could know what he was thinking was to look into his eyes and try to read what was going on there. But she still didn't have the courage to do that.

'You could have been a queen.' His voice was rough and ragged. 'You turned down a kingdom—for what?'

For love.

But she didn't dare to say it.

'I didn't want it. I don't think I'm cut out to be a queen.'

'I would be proud to have you as my queen.'

Clemmie felt as if her head was about to explode. Had he really said...?

But Karim was moving, lifting her from her position against his chest, turning her so that from not daring to look into his eyes, she now couldn't look anywhere else at all.

'Why didn't you come to me?'

Oh, she'd thought about it. But she hadn't been able to bring herself to do it. If she and Karim were to have any future then he had to come to her of his own free will. Because he wanted to. Her heart wedged up high in her throat at the thought that he had done just that. But was there more than *wanting* behind his appearance here?

'Because you would have felt honour-bound to marry me, knowing that my reputation was ruined.'

She was right about that, Karim's slow nod acknowledged silently.

'Is that how you wanted it?' she asked sharply. 'That I would come running to you?'

'You told me that you loved me. Was that not true?'

Clemmie pulled away from him, wrapping the blanket tighter around herself, needing it like a suit of armour to hold her together when she feared she might start to crumble from the inside. Defiantly she lifted her chin, held her jaw as tight as she could.

'I told you that I loved you but you said nothing in return. Except to hold on tight to your honour. Was I supposed to take what little you had to offer—take this—?'

A wild wave of her hand indicated the tumbled blankets, the crumpled cushions where the scent of their mingled bodies still lingered. The gesture threatened her grip on the concealing blanket but she suddenly found she didn't care.

'And not ask for more because I loved you.'

'Loved?' Karim questioned and Clemmie didn't know how to answer him. She didn't even know how the question was being asked. Was it possible that he believed her love had not been as strong as she had declared it to be?

'Less than one week, Clemmie—is that all the time your love lasted?'

He almost sounded as if he was teasing her. And yet there was a rawness to his voice, a searching look in those deep dark eyes, that caught her up sharp and left her wondering…

'It was more than you gave me. More than you have for me…'

He closed his eyes for a moment as he shook his head and when he opened them again she felt the look he gave her go straight as an arrow to her heart.

'No, Clemmie. It wasn't like that. I didn't know what was happening to me. That night—that first night we spent here—you got under my skin and I've never been able to free myself from you. That night was the closest thing to crazy I have ever been, and I haven't felt in control of anything since. I had made a vow to my country—to my father—and I had to keep it. I had to walk away. By doing that, I kept my honour, but I lost you.'

Lost. It was such a small word but such a strong, emotive one, a world wrapped up in just four letters.

'And then I heard that you had defied Nabil—that you'd told him there was someone else. I could only pray it could be me. I had to come—to see if you still felt the way you had then.'

I have travelled halfway across the world for this. I have no intention of giving up now.

But he still hadn't said what *this* was.

'You came for someone who has lost her reputation?' Her voice wobbled dangerously on the words. 'What will that do for your so important honour?'

Karim's shake of his head was a violent rejection of her bitter question, the flash of rejection that accompanied it.

'I don't care about honour any more when I'm with you.'

'And you expect me to believe you?'

Once more those black eyes dropped to the tangled bed, then came back over her half-covered body, up to her face, warm as a caress.

'So what was that just now? And all the night long…?'

'That—that was just sex.'

'Just sex?'

Karim's voice had dropped an octave, deep and disturbingly sincere as he took her hand.

'For me, that will never be *just* anything. Not with you. And isn't there a line in the wedding service—*with my body I thee worship*. What is worship if not honour? I want to honour you—to worship you with my body for the rest of my life if you will let me.'

He lifted the hand he held to his mouth, turned it so that he could press a kiss against her palm. The gentleness of the caress tore at her heart and she knew that this was what she wanted for the rest of her life too.

'Clemmie…' Over her hand, Karim looked deep into her eyes. 'Will you let me? Will you marry me?'

She didn't want to ask the question but it had to be said. If he didn't answer it with the words she needed then how could she marry him, no matter how much she loved him? She had only just escaped from the prospect of one loveless marriage, so how could she ever tie herself down in another one?

'As…as a matter of honour?'

She'd thought—hoped—prayed that he would say no but instead he inclined his head in a slow, thoughtful nod.

'Yes, as a matter of honour…but not in the way you mean it.'

'What other way is there? Your honour demands that we should marry and so…'

And so she could never agree. Because she wanted more—needed so much more. But deep inside there was a weakness, a shadow on her heart that urged her to say yes.

'Not *my* honour.' Karim's tone was deep and dark, huskily intent. 'My honour no longer matters in this. What matters is the honour that you would do me if you agreed to be my bride. I can think of no other woman I could ever want as much. No other woman I could ever love as much.'

Love. That small, softly spoken word caught on her nerves and hung there, making her head reel. Could she really believe—had he actually said…?

'Love?'

'Yes, love,' he assured her. 'I love you and I have done almost from the moment that we met. I knew it when you climbed out of that window and went to Harry—and, in spite of everything my training had taught me, I waited. I waited for you to come back as you'd promised you would. I knew you would—I wanted you to come back. I wanted you.'

It was a low caressing whisper, sincerity in every word he spoke.

'I wanted you more than any woman I had ever met—

but it was more than that. I wanted you to be free to be the woman you really were. We were trapped in a situation that we couldn't control. Your father's scheming, those political treaties, my family's debt of honour had us trapped. I couldn't set us free—you were the only one who could do that when you told Nabil the truth.'

Reaching out, he touched her face, cupping her cheek softly in the palm of his hand, so that she could feel the faint tremor in his fingers that told her just how much he meant this.

'Clementina, you are my love, my honour. You are all I want out of life. All I need. But without you I am nothing. I love you and I want to do so till the end of my days. So please, tell me that your love is still there. Please say that you will marry me and make the rest of my life complete.'

And there was only one possible way she could answer that. Leaning her head to one side, she pressed her cheek against his hand and smiled deep into his eyes.

'I will, my love,' she told him, strong and sure. 'It will be an honour to be your wife.'

* * * * *

A sneaky peek at next month...

MODERN™

POWER, PASSION AND IRRESISTIBLE TEMPTATION

My wish list for next month's titles...

In stores from 20th June 2014:

- ❏ Christakis's Rebellious Wife — Lynne Graham
- ❏ Carrying the Sheikh's Heir — Lynn Raye Harris
- ❏ Dante's Unexpected Legacy — Catherine George
- ❏ The Ultimate Playboy — Maya Blake

In stores from 4th July 2014:

- ❏ At No Man's Command — Melanie Milburne
- ❏ Bound by the Italian's Contract — Janette Kenny
- ❏ A Deal with Demakis — Tara Pammi
- ❏ Wrong Man, Right Kiss — Red Garnier

Available at WHSmith, Tesco, Asda, Eason, Amazon and Apple

Just can't wait?

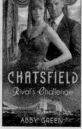

THE CHATSFIELD®

Enter the intriguing online world of
The Chatsfield and discover secret
stories behind closed doors…

www.thechatsfield.com

Check in online now for your exclusive
welcome pack!

MILLS & BOON® Book Club

Join the Mills & Boon Book Club

Want to read more **Modern**™ books?
We're offering you **2 more** absolutely **FREE!**

We'll also treat you to these fabulous extras:

- ❧ **Exclusive offers and much more!**

- ❧ **FREE home delivery**

- ❧ **FREE books and gifts with our special rewards scheme**

Get your free books now!

visit www.millsandboon.co.uk/bookclub
or call Customer Relations on 020 8288 2888